The Pathfinder

His Searchers

Book 2

By

Ronna M. Bacon

Proverbs 3:6

In all your ways, acknowledge him and he shall direct your paths. (NKJV)

Psalms 16:11 - Thou wilt shew me the path of life: in thy presence is fulness of joy; at thy right hand there are pleasures for evermore. (NKJV)

Table of Contents

$$Chapter\ 1$$

Shading his eyes with one hand against the bright sun reflecting off the lake, Conor Fitzsimmons studied the area. He had taken his accrued vacation, much against his will. He had been given no choice. Working the cases of close friends lately had drained him. Brownie, as he was affectionally known as, was worn out and beaten down. He needed to get his head straight again to continue with his career as a patrol officer. Today, that work was behind him.

His hand running through the close-cropped black curls, Brownie turned to study the area around him. He was on his own and that was what he wanted. Just him and God, he thought. He drew in a deep breath, relishing the smell of the fresh air. His deep blue eyes sought the woods that crept towards the lake, not quite reaching it. It was a favourite area of his, one that he could reach easily from his home even just for a day.

Brownie sighed once more, something that he felt he had been doing a lot of lately. He was at a crossroads, he knew, with his life and career. Seeing friends meet the ladies of their dreams, even in the midst of adversity and near death had him searching for his own. Only he couldn't find that one lady of his dreams.

Turning back towards the lake, Brownie reached for his canoe, sliding it ahead of him into the lake and then seating himself. A paddle in his hands, he paused, a sudden sense of danger coursing through him. He raised his eyes once more to the sky, praying for protection. He had a deep trust in God, having felt His presence in so many ways and at so many times.

Paddling across the lake and then following the shore towards a river, Brownie breathed in the fresh scents of the forest. The sounds of the late summer/early fall day filled his ears. He raised his eyes to watch the V-shaped formation of the geese in the sky. He smiled, the first genuine smile he thought in days.

"God, I know that You are here. I can see Your handiwork." Brownie could feel God around him. "I need to be renewed, only I don't know how. Only You can do that. This next month? Let me rest in You. Renew my spirit."

Brownie found a place to camp for the night or so. After setting up his tent and sorting out what he needed, he found a rock to sit on, his eyes on the forest on the other side of the river. He felt content and reached for his Bible. A frown crossed his face as he heard a noise.

On his feet, Brownie searched the area, moving towards the woods behind him. This was not what he expected, to hear another human voice. A female at that. He tilted his head to listen to the sweet alto raised in song.

He stood, watching the young woman, no lady, he thought, as she knelt at a rock pile. He frowned once more, before moving forward.

"Are you all right?" His deep bass voice sounded loud in the quiet of the forest and he winced.

"I am. I knew you were there." The lady was on her feet, turning towards him. "I'm sorry if I disturbed you." She gestured to the rock pile. "This is a tradition for my family in the late fall. We would bring a rock from our garden and place it here. It's a memorial to my family." She blinked back tears for a moment. "I'm Keegan Taylor."

"And I'm Conor Fitzsimmons. Friends call me Brownie." He stopped beside her, his eyes on the rock pile. "This is a nice memorial."

"Yes, it is." Keegan's eyes were on Brownie. "You've been through a rough patch in the last while, haven't you?"

Brownie turned surprised eyes to her, before he nodded.

"I have been. But how did you know?"

She shrugged, her long wavy auburn hair moving with the motion. Her deep brown eyes had compassion.

"I have a friend who knows you. Flannery."

"Flannery? Of course. Evan's wife. They are good friends." Brownie looked around, suddenly uncomfortable. "How did you get here, Keegan?"

"I walked. It's not really that far. At least most days." She looked around in sudden fright.

"You're frightened. Come with me." Brownie reached for her hand, tugging her with him, and then he slid to a stop. "Who's after you?"

"After me?" Her voice rose in question, ending in a squeak. "No one that I know of."

"Someone is out here. And they're not very quiet." Brownie pulled her with him, taking off on a run. "Where can we hide?"

"Hide? Why?" Keegan's voice was rushed as she tried to speak while running. Her head was moving as she searched for a place to hide. "In here."

Brownie followed her deeper into the woods. He shoved her down, his body covering hers, his arms wrapped around their heads. He could hear the heavy footsteps that were trampling everything in their path. Two men, no, three, he thought.

Keegan lay still, barely breathing as she too listened. Her eyes slid closed. She recognized the one voice, someone she considered a friend. But obviously he wasn't.

Brownie shifted his weight to the ground, his head raised as he both listened and searched for the men. He felt Keegan's hand gripping his.

"Brownie? I know that one man. He's supposed to be a friend. I don't understand why he is out here."

"Looking for you. But why?" Brownie shot her a glance, looked away, and then his gaze returned to her. He frowned, something that he thought he had been doing a lot that day.

"I don't know. I haven't seen him in a couple of months. He was supposed to be working on the other side of the country." Keegan sat up, finding Brownie had not released her hand.

—

"Well, obviously he isn't." Brownie looked around and then was on his feet, pulling her with him. "We need to make it back to my camp. We'll get away."

"How can you be so certain of that?" Keegan protested even as she ran with him.

"I know we can." Brownie was already pulling down his tent and stuffing it away as Keegan worked to pack up what he had pulled out. "The canoe. We'll take that down the river. We should be able to make it."

In the canoe, Brownie shoved them off, heading down the river. He kept an eye out, knowing that Keegan was doing the same. This is when I wish I had my fellow officers here, he thought.

Keegan screamed as she felt the canoe rock and then tip over. She struggled to the surface, finding Brownie there, searching for her.

"Brownie?" She screamed as she saw the men standing on the riverbank, rifles pointed at them.

"Keegan? You're okay?" Brownie treaded the water, his arms moving to keep him afloat.

"I am, but we're in trouble." Keegan pointed behind him. "He's there. And they have rifles pointed at us."

Brownie nodded, having come to that conclusion.

"I guess then we must do what they want." His hand suddenly reached for hers and he pulled her underwater, kicking hard to move them down stream and away from the men.

Only, it didn't work out as he planned. He didn't see the rock that was in his way and his head slammed into it. Keegan reached for him as his body went limp and she struggled to pull him to the surface. She dragged him towards the shore, worried that he was not responding to her pleas to wake up and be all right.

The three men were waiting for them. One of the men waded in to grab Brownie by his underarms and drag him roughly to shore where his body was dropped onto the rocks. Keegan was on her knees, her hands searching for injuries. She looked up, her hair dripping water on her face. Horror crossed it as she recognized the other men.

"Why? What did I ever do to you?" Her voice broke as she tried to understand.

"You were you." Her supposed friend sneered at her. "You weren't supposed to live, you know that."

"What? What are you talking about?"

"That accident two years ago? The one where you were to be involved? You were to be on that ski trip. It was all arranged." Edwin Short sneered once more. "You were to die on the slopes. Just because."

"I don't get it, Edwin. What did I ever do?"

"Nothing. That's the thing. You were to disappear but were too well protected. You had to die because you cost me a lot of money. This is where you die." The rifle pointed at her head.

One of the other men stepped forward, and with a hand, forced the rifle downwards.

"This is not the time or place, Short. The boss wants to talk with her." He stared down at Brownie. "They both will work for him."

Keegan was forced to her feet and yanked harshly towards the forest. Her cries to leave her alone and let her help Brownie were ignored. Brownie was picked up and roughly dropped over one of the men's shoulders before they too disappeared into the forest.

There was no evidence left to show what happened, other than the paddle slowly floating down the river. No one knew where they were or what had happened to them.

Chapter 2

Keegan struggled to escape the hard grasp that the man had on her wrist, but was unable to do so. She kept trying to turn to keep an eye on Brownie but she was prevented from that as well. Keegan's fear grew as she was yanked towards a cave and then shoved roughly forward with enough violence that she landed on her hands and knees. The shock reverberated through her body, causing her to bite at her lips to keep the cries inside her.

Brownie's body was dropped beside her, his head hitting the stone floor in a sodden manner. Keegan crawled towards him, falling backwards as Edwin's foot shoved her shoulder. He laughed uproariously as she fell, a cry of pain drawn from her.

One of the older men shook his head, his eyes on Keegan. This was not part of the plan, he knew, that she be mistreated and harmed. His hand grasped Edwin's upper arm and he yanked him outside.

"Enough, Short. This is not going to go well with the boss if you keep hurting them." Walker, known only by his last name, was muscle for hire and had worked for his boss for a number of years. He was angry with Short and knew that his boss would be as well.

The other man, Baker by name, shook his head as well. He walked away, his phone out, frustrated that he could not get a signal. He turned back to

Walker, quietly letting him know that he was heading out to try and get a signal. Walker nodded, his eyes on Short.

"Watch him. He's out of control." Baker eyed Short.

"He is. I wasn't aware that he knew her or I would have asked that he not be involved." Walker was frustrated. They had a task to accomplish and Short was interfering in it.

"The boyfriend wasn't an element that we were aware of. She was to be on her own." Baker turned to face the cave entrance.

"He's not her boyfriend. At least, I don't think that he is. Last night, I was told that she had no one in her life. Her family is gone and she wasn't dating anyone." Walker had a sudden thought and headed back into the cave. He shoved Keegan to one side and felt for Brownie's wallet. He pulled it out and then looked for identification. His hand froze as he found it.

Baker stood beside him, a frown on his face as he stared at Walker and then at the identification in his hand.

"Walker? What's the problem?"

Walker looked up at Baker, a hard look on his face.

"He's a cop. We've got a cop in our midst and you know what that means."

Baker stared at him and then spun, his foot kicking a rock across the cave where it bounced off the wall and back towards him.

"A cop? How did he get involved?" Baker spun back towards Keegan and reached to grab a handful of hair. He pulled her upright by it, not listening to her cries to let her go, that he was hurting her. "How did that cop get here? Tell me?" He shook her by her hair, his eyes on Short as he appeared in the doorway.

"What's all the ruckus?" Short, for a moment, appeared confused.

"He's a cop, Short. What did you get us into?" Walker threw Brownie's wallet on his body and stalked toward Short. His hands clenched and unclenched. "What did you do?"

"Me? I did nothing. I didn't know that man. And she certainly hasn't been dating anyone. I've been watching her." He didn't see the look of hatred and loathing directed towards him.

Walker shoved him from the cave and towards the river. Short was still protesting that Keegan was not dating anyone. The older man stared at him, stared across the river, and then raised his rifle. A single shot and the river claimed a victim, the water staining red as Short's body hit it and then floated downriver, facedown. Walker had no compunction about shooting him. It wasn't the first man or woman for that matter that he had killed and wouldn't be the last. It was his duty to remove obstacles to his boss' wishes, and Short had become a huge one.

Baker was waiting outside the cave, his eyes on the river.

"No choice." His words were few.

—

15

"No, he was just trouble. I don't know what the boss saw in him, but now we need to move these two. Is he awake?"

"No, he's not. And you know the cops will be looking for him. That's a given."

Walker sighed, knowing that his compatriot was correct in his guess.

"They will be. And one of us has to explain that to the boss."

"Yeah, we do. Listen. Stay here. I'm heading back towards our vehicle. I should be able to get service there." Baker walked away, leaving Walker staring at the river.

Walker had no regrets. Short had served his purpose and was no longer of any use. The boss would not question his actions, except to ask if he would have been of any further use.

Keegan huddled near Brownie, fear on her face. Her hand rested on his forehead, the extra T-shirt she was wearing pressed to the bloody lump there. Brownie had not roused and that frightened her. She needed him awake, alert, and on his feet. She had jumped in terror as she had heard the rifle shot, her eyes shooting towards the entrance, expecting that Brownie and she would be next. Her eyes sought Brownie and she suddenly felt for a pulse, scared that he was dead. She felt his chest rising and falling and drew a deep breath of relief.

Hearing footsteps behind her, she froze, not looking up. Keegan was too scared for that. This is when her father would have told her to trust God, that He was there and was looking out for her. Only, she didn't really feel His protection. If He wanted to protect her and Brownie, this would never have happened.

Walker stopped behind her, a closed look on his face as he watched Keegan and then Brownie. The boss would want them kept alive and forced to work for him. His various enterprises needed workers. It would be so appropriate that a cop would have to work for a criminal.

Chapter 3

Walker paced outside of the cave, waiting for Baker to return. Being out in the wilderness was not his thing, he decided. He wanted to be back where he had asphalt and sidewalks under his feet and the only danger came from himself. Looking up at the sky, Walker noted the darkening of the day. Rain was moving in and he wanted to be under shelter.

Baker appeared beside him, his footsteps as quiet as he could make them. He didn't speak, waiting for Walker to do so.

"What did he say?" Walker didn't look at Baker, his eyes on the river, a contemplative look on his crime-hardened face.

"He wants them at the building. He'll put them to use. He's not happy that the cop was hurt and might die on us."

"Yeah, well there is that." Walker turned to face the cave. "We'll need to move them then."

"He's okay with Short dead. He was ready to get rid of him. He said Short was a troublemaker."

"He always has been. Even as a kid." Walker's face hardened even more. "Let's get them moved then. I would rather not be out in the rain. Which building?"

"The Woods' one."

Walker nodded. "It's near where the guys are cutting the walnut trees. He'll work there. She can too."

Walker strode into the cave, stopping behind Keegan. Keegan didn't look around as she huddled over Brownie, an arm around him to try and keep him warm. With the rain moving in, the air had chilled in the cave. Her clothing had dried from her soaking, but she was chilled. Her shivers shook her body as it tried to cope with the chilly air. Walker pulled her roughly to her feet, his hand tight on her wrist even as she struggled to escape. He ignored her protest at their treatment of Brownie. Baker hauled Brownie to his feet and then draped him over his shoulder, a frown that the younger man was still unconscious. This was not what they needed. The boss wanted him alive to work in the tree-cutting operation.

Keegan struggled to escape, twisting and turning her wrist. It just didn't break the grip. She was hauled through the woods, tripping and stumbling over the debris on the trail, barely able to keep her feet. She shot frantic glances behind her, seeing Brownie's arms flapping limply as Baker walked behind Walker and her.

Walker shoved her into the front seat of his truck, her hands bound behind her even as Baker dumped Brownie in the back seat. Keegan twisted enough so that she could watch him. Baker kept his eyes on her as he sat behind Walker. He frowned for a moment. This was not how it was meant to be. Only Keegan was meant to be with them. Now, what about this cop? If he didn't return, then his fellow officers would be looking for him and likely soon.

Keegan gave a cry of pain as she was pulled from the truck and then hauled across the rough ground to a rough cabin. She was shoved inside. Spinning, Keegan stood, her hands covering her mouth, horror and fear on her face as Brownie was once more dumped unceremoniously on the rough wooden floor.

"I need medical supplies. Please?" Keegan was begging and knew it.

Walker stared at her dispassionately and then nodded. He turned and left, leaving Baker standing just inside the door. Walker returned and dropped a box on the floor, his head nodding towards the door. The men left, the padlock clicking behind them. This place had been prepared for Keegan and had been for a number of weeks. When she felt herself being watched, she had been, the men looking for the perfect opportunity to nab her.

Keegan stared at the door, her thoughts muddled. *Why were they brought here? And just what did they want? God, are You there? Protect us, please. Help us to get away.*

Her attention returned to Brownie. Keegan rifled through the box and then was on her feet, searching the cupboards for cloth. Please, Lord, let there be running water as she reached for the tap. It was only cold water but it would have to do, just for once.

Back on her knees, she gently wiped at the blood, winced as Brownie moved restlessly, trying her best not to hurt him any more than he had been hurt. He groaned as his eyes fluttered open and closed before he settled down once more, his head turning to the side. Keegan was worried and was on her feet again, shaking the door, trying the window, anything to find a way out. Only if she found a way out, how did she ever escape with Brownie unconscious? She searched the cabin once more, this time for a mug or glass or anything that she could find to get water into Brownie.

Night fell and with it darkness in the cabin. Keegan rubbed her hands up and down her arms, trying to warm herself. She rose, knowing there was a stove and stumbled towards it, opening the lid and reaching for kindling. She fumbled around the counter, hitting a small box and then shaking it. Matches, she thought. *God, is this You?* She struck one and watched carefully as the kindling and papers that she had crumpled up on top of them caught fire and then added small pieces of firewood. Hopefully, she thought, this will warm up the cabin,

She was back beside Brownie, a hand reaching for his face, feeling for a fever. She breathed a sigh of relief when she found it cool.

"Lord, please heal Brownie. I need him on his feet. We need to get away and we can't. Please, Lord?"

Chapter 4

His head turning, Brownie fought to regain consciousness. His eyes shot open as he did so, staring into the early morning gloom. He didn't know where he was. All he knew was that he had a violent headache and didn't know why.

Brownie sat up cautiously, his hand to his head before he rose to his feet. His eyes half-closed against the pain, he made his way to the rough ensuite. Coming back out into the room, Brownie studied it, not sure where he even was.

His feet not working as they should, he moved to the door and tried to open it, finding he couldn't. He moved to the windows and found them barricaded as well. How did he get out?

Brownie slumped to the floor again, his back to the wall, his eyes closing against the pain. He slept, not hearing any sounds around him. He didn't hear or see the door open and Walker appear.

Walker stood inside the door, watching first Brownie and then Keegan. This is not how it was to go, he thought once more. Brownie wasn't to be there, only Keegan. He looked around and then walked back out of the door and locked it. The bag of food and water was dropped to the floor just inside the door.

Keegan roused as she heard the door closing, fear driving her to her feet. She spun in a circle, terror on her face, not finding Brownie where she had last seen him. Where had he gone? Did those monsters have him?

Spying the bag on the floor, Keegan cautiously approached it, peering inside to find the food. She sighed. I guess this is really happening, isn't it, Lord? She lifted out the sandwiches and placed them on the counter, not sure how she would get Brownie to eat one. The water bottles followed. Keegan uncapped one and drank deeply, her eyes searching once more through the dimness of the cabin before she spied Brownie and then was across the room to kneel beside him. Her hands reached to touch him, shaking him gently.

Keegan could not rouse him, no matter what she tried. She slumped beside him and leaned her head against his shoulder. Lord, I need him to wake up and he just isn't. She roused a while later, on her feet to return to sit beside Brownie with a water bottle. He was sitting, slumped forward, and she needed to raise his head. His head hung down and his arms were resting limply in his lap. She was able to get him to swallow before his eyelids flickered.

Brownie raised his head, squinting against the light. His head was pounding, making it difficult to see or even think. He heard a voice calling him by name. Only, he didn't know the voice.

Keegan wrapped an arm around him and held the water bottle to his mouth. He swallowed and then laid his head back against the wall. His head hurt too much to even think. Brownie could feel soft hands on his face and then a gentle patting where his head hurt the most.

"Brownie? Can you hear me?" Keegan was in tears, scared beyond anything that she had ever been. "Brownie? Please wake up. I need you too."

Brownie groaned as he awoke even more. His head was pounding and he felt for the sore spot. He felt a soft hand reach to grasp it and pull it away. Brownie looked around through narrowed eyes. He didn't know where he was.

"Brownie? Can you look at me?" Keegan's hand gently turned him to face her. "Can you see me?"

Brownie squinted and then nodded, regretting it instantly.

"Who are you? And where are we?"

"I'm Keegan. You're Brownie. And we were kidnapped and brought here."

"We were? Why?" Brownie leaned forward, resting his head on his upraised knees.

"I don't know. We tried to get away but couldn't. You hit your head on a rock in the river and haven't really been right in the head since then. That happened yesterday. They've been around, I think, leaving us food. Can you eat?"

Brownie raised his head and sighed, a groan drawn from deep within.

"I don't think so." His head went back against the wall once more and he was lost to Keegan.

Keegan watched with concern, knowing that Brownie needed medical attention and wasn't likely to get it. She wrapped an arm around his and her head went down on his shoulder. She dozed off. She hadn't had a lot of sleep the night before, her sleep broken with fear and her worry about Brownie.

Neither one saw the door fly open and bang against the wall. They both jumped but didn't awaken. Walker stood watching them, dislike and hatred on his face. The boss would be around the next day and Walker needed them on their feet. And that didn't appear that would happen.

Baker appeared in the doorway, frowning as well.

"They're not awake?"

"No, and they need to be. Come on. We'll come back later. I need to head out to see how much timber has been cut."

"That you do. I'll be around. I'll check on them later."

Chapter 5

The next day, Brownie was hauled to his feet and shoved out of the door, barely able to walk for his feet stumbling over one another. He was forced to walk about half a mile to where the men were working cutting the walnut trees. He stood, swaying, his head pounding. Brownie blinked to clear his vision.

Walker watched him, frowning heavily. His eyes raised to the men working and then moved back to Brownie.

"Here. You start working. Clean up the area." Walker shoved Brownie forward once more, not caring that the other man landed on his hands and knees.

Keegan had stood, shock on her face that Brownie was removed before she was at the door, hammering at it as hard as she could. She tugged at the handle, finding the door locked. She ran for the windows, frantically trying to open them, but couldn't.

"Please, let me out. Let me go with Brownie. He's not well enough to be out there. Please?" Keegan was back at the door hammering at it. "Please? Let me go with him?" Sobs coloured her voice and tears covered her face.

Keegan paced the cabin all that day, worry for Brownie uppermost in her mind. She spun as the

---

door opened in the late afternoon. Brownie was shoved forward to land on his hands and knees once more. That seemed to have been a common position he had found himself in over the day.

Brownie was exhausted. The work that he had been forced into had not been that hard but with his injury, it had been very difficult. Keegan stared at him and then at Baker as he stood watching them, a gloating look on his face.

The door slammed as Keegan watched. She was over beside Brownie almost before it was, on her knees, her arms wrapped around him.

"Brownie? Are you all right? Brownie? Talk to me, please." Sobs choked her voice, sobs that she hated but couldn't control.

Brownie raised his head, pain evident on his face. It had been a brutal day. He had been allowed few breaks, Walker making sure that he didn't stop for very long. His head was pounding once more and all he wanted to do was sleep.

"I'm okay, Keegan, is it?" He was having trouble with his short-term memory at that point.

"It is, Brownie." Keegan looked around, on her feet to find water for him, and a cloth to wash his face. "Here, Brownie. Drink. You need to."

Brownie finally gave a brief nod, shifting his weight to a sitting position. For once, he wished that he wasn't so tall, over six foot. He reached for the bottle of water, uncapping it and sipping at it. He raised his eyes to study Keegan, finding her sitting tight to him, a hand on his shoulder.

—

"Keegan? What happened to you today? Are you okay?" Brownie was concerned about her. He studied her deeply.

"Nothing. Absolutely nothing. I was just locked up in here. But what about you?" Keegan touched his hand lightly. "You look like you did hard work."

"I did. They're logging walnut trees illegally and I was forced to clean up the area." He sighed, a deep from-the-toes sigh. "We're in the hands of criminals, Keegan. I heard them talking. They were after you but I don't know why. I need out of here to investigate."

"Brownie? What? Investigate? You can't do that. You're not a police officer!" Keegan was shocked at his words.

"But I am, Keegan. I'm on vacation for a month but I need to get out of here and find out what's going on."

"Well, we can't." Keegan leaned harder against him, wrapping an arm around his, repeating the action that she had taken previously. "So, what do we do?"

Brownie's eyes slipped shut as he prayed. God was the only One Who could get them out of there. Only he had no idea when or how.

"I know, Keegan. I know. I just wish I could remember what happened but I don't."

Keegan shot a look at the door, not sure if one of the men might be returning.

"What did they make you do today?"

"Clean up, like I said. I don't like it, Keegan. They're stealing the lumber and selling it on the black market." Brownie kept his voice low, not sure if the cabin had been bugged or not.

"They are? But where does that leave you if you're helping?" Keegan was suddenly worried. "Does God even care?"

"He does, Keegan. Very much. He has a purpose for this. He will never leave us. There may be paths that we have to walk and He goes before us."

Keegan thought about that.

"You're right, but I just don't see how we can get out of here. You're not well enough to walk too far without falling over."

Chapter 6

Three weeks went by, three weeks that brought no relief. Brownie was made to work every day, cleaning up the sites. His headaches had decreased and he was regaining his strength. He worried about Keegan, watching as the strain of being locked away all day, every day, was drawing on her strength. Brownie was desperate to get her away and free but there was never an opportunity.

Brownie turned that day, watching the men working, knowing that Baker was watching him. He only had a week left before he was to report back as a patrol officer and he just didn't know how that would happen. If he didn't report in, then his friends and co-workers would be looking for him. A sudden thought crossed his mind and he needed to talk to Keegan. Only it would have to wait.

Keegan didn't turn to face him that night as he was locked back into the ramshackle cabin. She kept her face to the window, a dejected slump to her shoulders. Brownie watched and then lifted his eyes up to the ceiling. *Lord, what is going on? What happened today? Something has.*

Brownie washed as best he could with the limited facilities and then moved to stand behind Keegan. His hands clenched and unclenched before he reached for her shoulders, just resting his hands there. He waited for her to speak, feeling the

—

shuddering in her body. Brownie knew that she was crying and likely had been for a while. He gently turned her to face him, gathering her close and just holding her as she broke down. Brownie couldn't begin to understand how she felt. He began to pray for her but this time, his prayer didn't calm her as it usually did.

Keegan's eyes closed as she heard Brownie praying. This time? She didn't feel the peace that he always prayed for. Today had destroyed that, she thought, and almost destroyed her. She didn't think that they would ever be freed. Baker had been around that morning, standing watching her.

Walker had shoved open the door, letting it fall violently against the wall. He had stood just inside the doorway, watching her. Kegan had backed away, to stand against the counter in the kitchen. She grew afraid. What did he want? He never came here during the day. She saw no one from when Brownie left until he returned, exhausted at the end of the day.

His eyes intent on her, Walker had smirked. He could see the fear that she was trying so hard to hide. That wouldn't work, he knew. The boss had been around. Decisions had been made about these two. They were due to move on to another site in a week and these two were going with them. The plan was to involve Brownie more and more into the illegal activities. Keegan? She would be the housekeeper, cleaning and cooking for them all. These two were not going anywhere.

"You're not going away, lady. You're moving when we move the end of the week. You will work for us, just like your man is." He sneered as he said the words, stood studying her reaction and then locked the door behind him.

Keegan stood, shock and fear on her face, her arms wrapping around her abdomen. What did he mean? Go with them? No, they couldn't do that. She had to find a way to get Brownie away. It didn't matter about her.

Brownie had startled her when he approached at the end of his work day. She didn't realize that time had passed so quickly. She had been lost in thought, trying to figure out a way to get Brownie free and away from here.

Wrapped in Brownie's arms, Keegan felt safe for a moment before she broke down in sobs. His arms tightened around her even as his head rested on top of hers. Brownie didn't say anything, just prayed for her.

"Keegan? What happened today?" Brownie spoke at last.

Keegan drew in a deep breath. She didn't want to speak but she knew that she had to.

"Walker was here. Did you know that they are planning on moving to a new spot next week?"

Brownie sighed. He had overheard the men saying that.

"I had heard that today. Why?"

"Because they are going to make us move with them. They're not letting us go. And I don't know why."

"Nor do I." Brownie drew her down to a sitting position, keeping his arm around her. "We'll get away. I'm strong enough now that we can do that."

"Do you know where we are?" Keegan finally looked at him, a frown on her face as she saw a look in his eyes, one that she was afraid to acknowledge but one that she had prayed to see in a man's eyes as he looked at her. "We need to get away, Brownie, but how?"

"God will provide a way, my darling. He has walked this path before u and will lead us along it. I know that you are scared. So am I." Brownie grew silent, praying, even as he felt Keegan gradually relax against him. He glanced down. She was asleep, feeling safe as he held her, something he wanted to do for the rest of his life. Keegan was wriggling her way deep into the recesses of his heart, into the part that he held for the love of his life and his soul mate.

Chapter 7

Six days later, Brownie was shoved roughly back into the cabin. He spun, just managing to stay on his feet. He had been told that they were moving the next day to another location. He was not ready to do that. Brownie felt Keegan's hand on his back and then her arms wrapping around him.

"Brownie? What happened?"

Brownie sighed, turning to wrap his arms around her in turn.

"We're moving tomorrow. And I just can't do it that to you. We need to find a way out of here tonight. Only I don't know how." Brownie moved away, searching the cabin once more. There had never been any furniture brought it. They had had to sit and sleep on the floor. The kitchen was empty of any utensils, pots, pans, and dishes. Keegan had struggled, he knew, with that. His eyes rested on the wood stove and then the kindling stacked beside it. He reached for the largest piece that he could find and hefted it in his hand. It would work, he decided. He knew that either Baker or Walker would be back that night, just to stand and gloat.

Keegan watched from the dirty window that overlooked the driveway, a frown on her face as she watched the vehicles leave, all but one.

"Brownie? They're leaving. All of them but Baker." She felt Brownie's hand on her back as he moved quickly to her side. "Are they not waiting for tomorrow?"

"I guess not. That's all the men." He paused, his hand gripped around the piece of wood. "Baker is still here." He looked desperately around, trying to find a way out that they had not found before. "We need to leave and leave now."

A rattling at the door had them spinning to stare at it and then at one another. Baker stumbled in. It was obvious that he had been drinking.

"We're leaving now. Not tomorrow." He pointed at them and then grew angry when neither one moved. "I said, move and move now!"

Brownie tucked Keegan behind him and carefully approached, the piece of wood hidden at his side.

"We're not going anywhere. Not with you." Brownie paused just out of reach of Baker. He nodded. A simple shove would take him down. "Keegan, run!" He grabbed at her and shoved her towards the door.

Keegan ran, her breath catching in fear at she evaded Baker's reach. Brownie was behind her, a simple shove sending Baker to the floor. Pausing, Brownie felt for car keys, not finding any. That puzzled him for a moment before he was through the door, slamming it behind him, and then snapping the lock shut. The key was left in and likely had been all along, he thought. Reaching for Keegan's hand, he pulled her towards the garage.

Keegan tried to keep to her feet, her head turning to watch the cabin.

"Brownie?" Her voice was barely audible. "Baker?"

"He's okay. Knocked himself out is all. I'm sure someone will be back for him." Brownie's eyes were searching for a vehicle. "I see one."

Brownie was at the car, tugging at the door but not able to open it. He leaned against the glass, his hands cupped around his face to see inside. No keys, he thought. He spun to stare around the garage.

"Brownie? Can you ride a bike?" Keegan was at his side, tugging at his arm.

"A bike? What are you talking about?" He turned to watch her before he lifted his eyes to where Keegan was pointing. "A dirt bike? Yeah, I can. I mean, I haven't in years, but Dad and I used to ride with a friend of his and his daughter."

"Okay, let's go." Keegan scampered away, looking for helmets. She found two, holding them aloft in victory. "Here, Brownie. Will it run?"

"We'll soon see." Brownie checked for fuel and then nodded. "The tank is full. Come on. Let's move away from here."

"Do you even know where we are?" Keegan followed Brownie closely as he wheeled the dirt bike away from the property.

"Not really. Did you remember anything?" Brownie watched her for a moment.

"No. I was too scared and too worried about you." Keegan waited as he started the bike before he jumped on. She was on the seat behind him, her arms wrapped around him, as he paused to pray for them. "Where do we head?"

Brownie sat for a moment, contemplating her question and then praying. God, You need to lead in this. I don't know exactly where we are. I have an idea, but please, Lord? Guide us to safety.

Brownie took off, Keegan hanging on tighter. She prays that he knew where he was going but she had her doubts. Her prayer was that Brownie knew where he was.

Pausing for a moment, Brownie searched the night sky, trying to find his way. Then he knew exactly where they were and just where he had left his truck. Only, he didn't know if it would still be there after almost four weeks.

He drew up to the hidden area that he had found and searched. He breathed a sigh of relief. His truck was still there. Brownie had been sure that it was gone, towed away. But the friend who had directed him there hadn't expected Brownie to return until the next day. He would have been around then to check on Brownie if he hadn't heard from him before that.

Keegan hopped off, shock on her face as she saw the truck, before she turned to Brownie.

"Brownie? What is this?"

"My truck. I left it here the day we were abducted. My friend could have been around tomorrow to see if I had left. Okay, so we put this bike in the back. Jump in." He handed her his keys. "It won't take long."

—

As good as his word, Brownie had the bike safely tied down in the back and was behind the wheel, reaching for the keys but instead grasping Keegan's hand. He studied her, finding that she was studying him in return. He smiled before he reached to kiss her cheek.

"Thanks for being such a good sport. You triumphed through all this." Brownie sat back, his eyes on the windshield, not seeing her look of surprise and then the softening of her face.

Brownie, what am I to do with you? Keegan found that Brownie had begun to work his way into her heart at well.

"We'll head towards my place. We need to talk, Keegan, but right now, we need to get to safety." Brownie reversed his vehicle and then sped off, heading towards his home and safety, he prayed. Only it not likely was. He was certain that the men knew who exactly he was and where he lived. Brownie needed to get Keegan to safety. Only, he didn't want to let her go. She had become that important to him. Biting at his lip, Brownie sorted through his ideas and knew that only one would work for him. But would it be for Keegan?

Chapter 8

Keegan stepped through the door into the house, not sure what was happening. It was now really late at night and she was dropping with exhaustion but also with hunger. Brownie searched his home, coming back to stand in front of her, biting at his lip. He was uncertain, not at all the calm and certain officer that he normally was. This was different. This time? He had brought a lady to his home and knew that he should have taken her somewhere else. Only, he had no idea where that was.

"The house is okay, Keegan. A little stuffy from being closed up. Look, you'll want to shower or bath or something and wash your hair." He turned for a moment, biting once more at his lip, staring down the hallway. "There's a bedroom that you can use. My sister uses it when she's here. I think that she has left some clothes there. She would tell you to use them."

Keegan stared at him for a moment before she nodded. Cleaning up and getting into clean clothes sounded so wonderful. All she wanted to do with the ones she was wearing was burn them.

"Ok. Which room?"

Brownie swung an arm around her and led her to the spare bedroom.

"It has an attached bath. The clothes are in the drawers. Take and use what you need to. Cami won't mind." Brownie pulled the door closed, his head resting back on it. Lord, we need to make some decisions and I am not sure how Keegan will react.

He headed for the kitchen, squinting at the clock. Not that late, he realized. His phone was out and plugged in to recharge. He could only imagine the number of text messages and voice mail messages that he would have. Brownie needed to call his supervisor but elected to send a text message when he had enough of a charge to do just that. Justin Landon, his supervisor, would respond as quickly as he could, that Brownie knew. Brownie also knew that there was no way that he would be reporting for duty on the next day. He wouldn't be allowed to. There would be medical appointments to assess his physical and mental health.

Reaching into the freezer, Brownie pulled out a container of soup that his mother had put there just before he went on vacation. A loaf of bread followed. He paused, his head turning towards the hallway before he walked that way. He needed to clean up as well and shave. It had bothered him, the beard that he had been forced to grow. He preferred a clean-shaven look, but that had not been possible. The two men holding them captive had seen to it that there were no razors available.

Fifteen minutes later, he was back in the kitchen, his hair roughly toweled dry, feeling more like himself, he thought. He worked to heat the soup and make sandwiches from the cheese that he had in the fridge. It would do for tonight, he thought, something warm and filling. The coffee had finished perking and he poured a cup for himself, inhaling the aroma of the freshly-ground beans that he used. He would wait to pour Keegan's, he thought.

His phone chimed at that moment, and he spun it to stare at the screen. Justin had been out when he sent his text but had responded. No, Brownie would not be reporting for work in the morning. Justin would be there at his place, mid-morning, to find out just what had happened and why Brownie had not been in touch.

A soft sound came from the doorway and Brownie spun, fear moving through him for a moment. Keegan stood hesitantly in the doorway, her eyes on him. Her hair was still wet from the shower. His hand was outstretched for hers.

"Feeling better?"

Keegan nodded. She looked down at her phone.

"I need to charge this."

Brownie took it, studied it and then found a charger for it. He pointed to the table.

"I have soup and sandwiches. I didn't think that we would want anything heavy tonight." He set their meal on the table, sat and then reached for her hand, his head bowing in prayer. He hesitated for a moment when he finished, his hand tightening on hers.

"Keegan? We need to talk but the morning will be okay. My supervisor will be here in the late morning to talk with us."

"I see. I'll be out of your hair in the morning, then." Keegan looked down at the bowl of soup, no longer hungry. Tears clouded her vision. She had begun to depend on Brownie and she just wasn't sure how to live without him.

"Keegan? I am going to ask you something. Take tonight to pray it over." Brownie bit at his lip, something he seemed to be doing a lot in the last few hours. "With us abducted and then kept the way that we were, people will talk. Not our friends or families. Without meaning to, your reputation has or may be damaged. I don't want that for you." Brownie paused once more, his eyes on the hand that Keegan had reached out to cover his. "Would you consider marrying me, just until we get this behind us? To save your reputation? I know it's not much and it's not right." He was on his feet, heading for the back door. "I'm sorry. Forget what I said."

Keegan stared at the back door, her hand covering her mouth. *Did he really just say that, Lord, and ask that of me? What do I say? I know what he means and that concerns me.* Her head dropped for a moment before she rose and began to clear away their meal. When she was finished, she ran her hands down the clothes that she was wearing. Leggings. An oversized T-shirt. Socks. There had even been unopened packages of undergarments. Keegan need to find his sister and thank her. She sighed even as she eyed the door. No, she couldn't go to him. He was right, she did need to pray over what he asked. It would be a long night.

Keegan sank gratefully onto the bed, pulling covers over her that made her feel snug and warm.

Only, they weren't what she wanted. She wanted back in that cabin, with the few blankets that they had been provided. For, you see, Brownie wasn't there and she needed that. She needed Brownie near her.

Brownie stepped through the back door, searching for Keegan. He sighed when he realized that she was not there. He could only pray that she was still in the house, tucked into her bed. He looked around, ready to tidy the kitchen, and stopped. Keegan had been busy, he thought. She did this, even though I walked outside. I need to do better.

His hand on his phone, Brownie unplugged the charger and headed for his bed. If there was not a life and death text message or voice mail, he would sleep. At least, that was his plan. Instead, he was awake for the night, bathing the love of his life in prayer, knowing that he did love her and afraid that she would walk away from him. His eyes found the message from his mother, just worried about him and asking how his time away had been. Could they meet tomorrow sometime, depending on his shift? His fingers hesitated before he sent a reply, stating that they needed to talk, that he had met someone, and no his time away had not been the fun and relaxing trip that he had needed. A simple reply of I love you, son, and we're praying was all she sent.

Chapter 9

Early the next morning, Brownie was on his feet, in his home office, methodically working through his voice mail and text messages. Most of them were easy to answer. It was the one from his father that he had difficulty with. His father, Cameron, had sent a lengthy text just that week, asking if Brownie was okay. He had been burdened for his son, driving by his home multiple times and even coming in and searching.

Brownie sat back. How did he answer his father? His father was a minister who had retired early to run a mission in his home town. Brownie bit at his lip. He needed his mom and dad there that day. Keegan had finally confided in him that her parents had walked away from her the day that she turned 18, telling her that she was on her own and not to come looking for them if she ran into difficulty. They had simply left her a letter, not even speaking with her He had simply held her as she wept. How a parent could do this? Brownie just couldn't understand that.

Brownie turned his phone over and over in his hands, his eyes on the doorway. He should be speaking to Keegan first, but he hadn't heard any movement from her. He didn't know if Baker had been found the night before. Brownie only knew that the two of them were in danger and he would do everything in his power to protect her.

"Hello?"

Brownie heard the early morning roughness of his father's voice and groaned to himself. He squinted at the clock. It was only 5 a.m.

"Dad? Sorry. I didn't mean to wake you."

"Not a problem, son. It never has been. You have only done this a handful of times and those were usually emergency situations. What is going on? You haven't been in touch for four weeks."

Brownie could hear the rustle of blankets as his father sat up and heard the quiet voice of his mother.

"I know, Dad. It's a long story, but the gist of it? I was kidnapped along with a beautiful lady and held captive until last night. We were able to escape and she's here with me."

"Only, you're worried about her and her reputation. I know you, Brownie. I know how you think. Listen. Don't say any more. Your mom and I will be right over. Let me pray with you first, Brownie. I fear that you are walking one of those paths that your friends have."

Brownie gave a bark of laughter.

"And that would be about right, Dad. Justin will be around later this morning. He's put me off duty for now, just until I can get some assessments done."

"Were you or the lady injured?" Brownie had heard his mother's voice asking that question.

"I was. A head injury that I think has healed. But it's Keegan that I am worried about. Something

—

was said to her yesterday that destroyed her. And her parents walked away from her when she was 18, told her not to contact them.”

“Oh, son! That’s heartbreaking. Listen, we’ll be there in twenty.” Cameron hung up the phone, turning to his wife, devastation showing briefly on his face.

Cara looked at him before she moved into his arms.

“How serious is this, Cam?”

“Very, I would say. They’ll be looking for Brownie and his lady. They likely know where he lives. But I don’t understand how it happened. He was heading out on his own, just to spend time with God and get refreshed.”

“I’m sure there is quite the story there. And we will get it from them.” Cara moved to dress, pausing for a moment. “She’ll need clothes, Cam. Let me see what I have here that we can take. Trudy left a whole bunch for the mission yesterday. God was working there, now wasn’t he?”

Brownie stood on the front porch of his bungalow a short time later, watching as his parents approached him. His father hugged him, holding on to his son as he prayed for him. Cam stood back, his hands on his son’s shoulders, seeing the tall, honourable man in front of him. Bless him, Lord. He wants to do what is right, what he has prayed about. That was the character of the man in front of him.

Cara watched her son, then moved in on him, her mother arms holding him tightly. Their relationship had changed over the last few weeks, that much she knew, but it was only right and natural.

"Brownie? Are you okay?"

"I am, Mom. At least, I think I am." Brownie swung an arm around her and turned her to the house. "I need you to meet someone."

"You do, do you? Here. Mom brought some clothes for Keegan, is it? Trudy had dropped off a bunch of new stuff." Cam set the back down in the hallway. "Now, what were you up to?"

"Me? Not much, at least for now." Brownie paused in the kitchen door. He hadn't heard Keegan as she had moved into the kitchen, starting their coffee and then searching for something to make for breakfast. "Keegan, my darling. You're up. Mom and Dad are here."

Keegan froze, her hands on the saucepan that she had pulled from the cupboard. Her eyes slid closed as she fought back tears. She just knew that they would blame her. Keegan jumped as she felt an arm around her and a mother's voice in her ear.

"Keegan, welcome, my dear. Brownie hasn't said much, other than that you two shared an adventure. One that you will need to tell us about. But first, we'll eat. Then, we'll pray."

Keegan relaxed against Cara, feeling the mother love that she hadn't felt in so many years. She nodded, reaching up a hand to swipe away her tears.

"Thank you." Her voice was low and barely audible. "That means a lot."

—

Cameron stood on her other side, his own arm around her.

"You are now a part of our family, love. Cara has taken you into her heart, just like that." Cameron shared a grin with his son. "Now, we'll eat and then pray. Mother brought breakfast with her, son. She knew that you wouldn't have a lot of fresh stuff, not yet. She's planning on shopping for you this morning."

"Thanks, Mom. This is great." Brownie moved in on Keegan and pulled her to one side, just holding her. His parents had reacted just as he had expected that they would. "Are you okay?"

Keegan shrugged, her eyes on Brownie.

"Brownie, how do we have that talk if they're here?"

Brownie simply turned her towards his office, leaving his parents to shoot speculative glances after them.

"It's okay. If I know Mom, it will be about thirty minutes for breakfast. She's doing one of her fancy ones." Brownie sat on his couch in the office, drawing Keegan down with him, and not letting go of her even as she tried to shift away from him. "Keegan, you are a beautiful, caring, compassionate, courageous lady. One I am honoured to call friend. For now, would you consider marrying me? Just until we get through what this is, whatever it is. We can get an annulment after. I just fear for you and don't want to see anything happen to you."

"But it still can." Keegan kept her eyes on Brownie, not sure if he was serious. Then, she sighed. "I thought this is what you meant. How do we do this? We're not in love."

Brownie simply grinned, causing her to frown at him.

"That's okay. I have friends who married to save one another. They are deeply in love. I'll introduce you to them and you can speak with the ladies. Only, I think we need to do this today."

"Today!" Keegan squealed in protest. "We can't. We'll never be ready."

"But you see, we can be. It won't take long to get the license. I can arrange flowers with a friend who is a florist. I'll book a private room at a fancy restaurant. Dad is a minister - he'll marry us and be glad to do it." Brownie looked around and was on his feet, moving from the room, returning with a small jeweller's box and a bag that his mother had handed him.

Back on the couch beside her, he reached for her hand, opening the box.

"Would you wear this? It was my Mom's as a young girl. She gave it to me for my bride."

Keegan blinked back tears, wishing her parents had been like Brownie's. She could only nod through her tears. Brownie simply slid the pink sapphire ring on her finger and reached to draw her close. He couldn't begin to understand how she was feeling.

"Mom brought her wedding dress. If you want. She just said God told her too."

—

Keegan looked up, staring at the beautiful gown that Brownie was holding up, barely able to see it through her tears. She simply nodded yes.

Chapter 10

Late that evening, Brownie moved quietly through his home. No, he thought, their home, his and Keegan's. How that had happened, he still wasn't sure, but he knew for certain that God had been there. His mother and father had simply welcomed her into his home, Cara coming in to do so as well. He prayed for his bride and the situation that they were in. Brownie still had no clear idea as to why.

Brownie turned and moved to the living room doorway, standing there and picturing Keegan as she had stood there, in his mother's dress. She is so beautiful, Lord. *Protect my lady, please. Help me to solve whatever it is that she is facing. I fear for her life.*

Justin had appeared in the early afternoon, not saying much at first. He had studied Brownie as he entered the home, sensing that Brownie was troubled.

Seated at the kitchen table, Justin took the mug of tea with thanks, a frown briefly showing on his face.

"Brownie? What happened? It's not like you to just disappear and then reappear, stating that you're not fit for work until you are medically cleared."

"No, it's not, Justin." Brownie rubbed at his forehead, a headache starting. He praised that it would only be mild this time. "I have seen the work physician. He wants to run some tests. With the headaches that I still have, he wouldn't clear me for a while. Besides, I need to take to someone about what happened to me."

"And what just did?" Justin shifted on his seat as he heard soft footsteps. A woman's, he thought. This is very odd. Who could she be?

Brownie was on his feet, reaching for Keegan as she hesitated in the doorway, drawing her to her seat at the table and then setting her juice in front of her.

"Brownie?" Justin spoke when Brownie didn't, a frown on his face as he saw the wedding bands on their fingers. "Who is the lady? And just what did you go and do?"

Brownie kept his eyes on Keegan, who watched Justin in return. He sighed to himself. This was not going to be easy. Any way that he did it? It meant Keegan could be hurt and that he wanted to avoid.

"Justin, this is Keegan. We shared an adventure over the last month. But most importantly, she is my bride."

"Your bride?" Justin drew in a deep breath. "I don't understand, Brownie. You never dated."

"No, I didn't. I didn't want a lady to think I would choose her for life. This is different. Keegan needed me and I needed her. God brought us together."

"Okay. Keegan, may I call you that? Thank you." Justin's eyes shifted between the young couple. "Brownie, talk to me. Tell me what happened."

———

"It's like this." Brownie hesitated before he wrapped his arm around Keegan, feeling her shuddering for a moment. "I went out to camp and instead found an adventure. I had made up my camp, found Keegan, and then we had to run for our lives. There were three men there. One of them shot at the canoe we were in, causing it to swamp. We tried to escape but when I dove underwater, I hit a rock with my head and knocked myself out. Keegan rescued me and then when we reached the shore, we were taken captive.

"I was made to work in an illegal logging operation, doing grunt work. Keegan spent her days locked up in a ramshackle cabin. It had nothing in it, except a few blankets. They kept us that way. We escaped last night, knocking out one of the men and then riding a dirt bike out to where my truck was. The rest is history, as you say. Keegan and I married, in part to keep her safe."

"Illegal logging?" Justin had begun to make notes. "We've had rumours of that but no real proof. Not until now. Brownie, we'll need the exact location of where you were."

"I have that all written down for you." Brownie was on his feet to his office and then back in his seat. "Here. We've written down everything as much as we can. I talked to Jason earlier and he was around and got our statements." Brownie was referred to one of the detectives on the force.

"Okay." Justin shot them both a look and then down at the folder. "Let me go through this and then we'll talk."

The only sound in the kitchen was the rustle of turning paper and the occasion sound of a pen as Justin made notes. Keegan was on her feet, glancing at the clock, working to prepare a simple meal for them. Brownie worked with her, knowing that Justin needed to read through what he had in front of him and think it through.

Keegan gathered up the dirty dishes and put away the food that was left. She turned to lean against the counter, her eyes on Brownie. He was in turn watching her, trying to assess what she was feeling. It had to have been an unsettling day for her, he thought, and then prayed for her.

"Brownie? This young man? Who is he? Was he there all the time? No, I see that he wasn't. What happened to him?"

"We don't know. Keegan said she thought she heard a gunshot but she can't remember. He just didn't show up at the cabin." Brownie reached out to shuffle through the paperwork. "I think it's in here that she said that."

Justin sat back. "How old?"

"I'm sorry?" Keegan shook her head. "I don't know what you mean."

"How old was this Short? Around your age? And how did you know him?"

"He's my age. We were in high school together. He hung around the edge of my group of friends. None of us liked him or really trusted him." Keegan stood with a hand on Brownie's shoulder. "Why?"

"About two days after you said that you were abducted, a group of youths, preteens, were at the beach where the river empties into our lake, Brownie. One of them, a young man, had been looking at the fish, following them, when he found what he thought was an old shirt. It was a body, of a young man."

"Short?" Brownie took a guess, his arm reaching to draw Keegan closer to him.

Justin nodded. "We could identify him from his wallet. We used dental records as well. He won't be troubling you anymore, but we do need to find the men responsible for his death as well as your abduction."

Keegan drew in a deep breath.

"He's dead? Then look for his brother, Edgar. They were always in trouble as teens. I don't think that they would have changed."

"I doubt it very much. Now, these two men?"

"Walker. Baker. I have no idea who they are. I don't remember seeing them before." Brownie wrinkled his forehead for a moment, deep in thought. "They were no amateurs at this. The trees? Black walnut and worth a lot on the black market."

"That they are. I'll hand this over to one of our detectives. They will be in touch with you." Justin sat back, his eyes on Brownie and then Keegan, who had seated herself once more after refilling their mugs. "Now, what can we do for you two?"

Keegan's mouth opened and closed, not sure what she should say. Brownie simply grinned at her.

—

55

"For starters, let the force know that I have married and provide that picture I gave you to them. They'll look out for us, Keegan. That is a promise. You're part of a family now."

"That you are, Keegan. Listen, I have to run. Emily has something on tonight that I need to be at. I'll be in touch tomorrow. Brownie, walk out with me, please."

Brownie stood for a moment on his front porch, watching as Justin drove away. They had a lot to think about, he thought. There needed to be an investigation and that was only in the preliminary stages, he knew. Keegan approached him, ducking under the arm that he used to draw her close to him.

"Brownie? What now?"

"What now? I see the medical people that we need to. We go to your home and pack it up, if that's what you want. What about your employment?"

Keegan gave a hard laugh.

"I don't have work. I had wanted to move on, only I had no idea where I wanted to go or what I wanted to do. Now, we're facing this. It doesn't help."

Brownie just hugged her tighter, dropping a kiss on her temple.

"That's okay. We'll figure it out. For now, you don't need to work. We need to find out what all is going on with this abduction and those men. There was more to it than what appeared on the surface with them."

"There is." Keegan moved away, to walk around the house, studying it and the gardens. She loved the gardens, anxious to dig into the dirt. Brownie had laughingly told her earlier that evening that they were hers to work in. He didn't know what was needed and trusted her completely.

Chapter 11

Two days later, Keegan slammed the front door, locking it and then standing against it, her breathing heavy as her hand rested on her chest. Walker had found them. He was standing outside the door, threatening her. She raced for her phone, calling for help. Brownie had gone to the station to speak with Justin about when he would return to work.

"Hey, Brownie?" The desk officer called to him as he was leaving. "We just caught a call from your wife. Something about someone named Walker?"

Brownie paled and then was gone, his feet pounding as he ran for his car. He could hear the sirens and see the lights ahead of him. He was out of his car, juggling his keys to find the right one, and slamming open the door, searching for Keegan. He found her huddled in his office, in a corner. Dropping to the floor, Brownie reached for her, finding her struggling against him until she realized it was him.

"Brownie?" The patrol officer stood in the doorway. "We don't see anyone around here now. Can we check your video feed?"

"We can. Keegan didn't imagine this, not after having to face that man for almost a month." Brownie looked up at that point, seeing puzzlement on the officer's face. "You see, Tim? We were

---

abducted and held captive for almost a month. Walker was one of those men."

Brownie rose, drawing Keegan with him, turning to his computer.

"Here, there's the feed from earlier today. And it is Walker. He's found us." Brownie was afraid for his bride.

"Him? He's been seen around town. He and another man." Tim turned to Brownie. "Justin said something about them."

"Yeah, they're the ones." Brownie's arm tightened around Keegan. "This is my wife, Tim. Keegan, this is a fellow officer, Tim."

"Okay, so, we'll look for him, but I doubt we'll find him today. He'll be hiding."

"I know. It worries me that he's been here. I can't be here with Keegan once I'm back on patrol."

"We get that, Brownie. You have always been there for any one of us who needed your help. We'll pick up for you. In fact, I would say that Keegan will be tired of seeing all of us. The ladies are planning to get together with you, Keegan. Sally, one of our fellow patrol officers, has asked if she can call you. Brownie, don't worry. We'll do all we can." Tim was gone at that.

Keegan stared at the doorway and then at Brownie, finding him rubbing at his upper lip, not quite able to hide his grin. Her eyes narrowed at him.

"Brownie, this is temporary, our marriage. They can't do this." Keegan was almost in tears. She

———

had longed for years to be included like this, only it had never happened.

Brownie swept her into his arms.

"It's what we do. Some will stand back, as they always do. But Sally? She's been a good friend. We grew up together. She'll make you feel part of this family." Brownie dropped a kiss on Keegan's forehead, drawing her eyes to him. "In fact, I have another friend here in town. We need to talk to her. She and her husband had an adventure, as did some other friends."

"They did? Like us?"

"Something like that. Ayron has been a good friend of mine since we were toddlers. Our parents were good friends. Her husband, Tag, was an officer until he retired and moved here."

"What is it with your friends? How many have had this happen to them?"

"Four of my friends. And others that I know of." Brownie turned her back into the office. "I need to contact someone and have her start a search on these two. She and her husband and the men on his security team went through some stuff. In fact, one of their friends, a fellow officer, and his wife have contacted me. Doug seemed to know something was up. His wife is a retired forensics psychologist but helps out friends as they need help."

"You have interesting friends, you know." Keegan gave a small squeak as she was pulled down onto Brownie's knee, bringing a quick grin from him. "What are you up to?"

"I am going to send an email to a friend, Evan. He works remotely for another friend, who has a company that tracks people. She's the one whose husband has the security team. Emma is really good at what she does, finding people and connections that not many other can find. We all tell her that her mind is scary." Brownie sat back. "Evan and his wife, Flannery, live just outside our town. We can actually go and visit them."

"We can't do that! What will they think?"

Brownie laughed, pointing to an email that he had just opened.

"That's from Flannery. She's already asking what I am involved in and why hadn't I called on them for help. Was I having an adventure like them?" Brownie continued to laugh, Keegan staring at him in shock. "Let me send off an email to her. Then, my darling, I want to take my bride out for lunch."

"Out for lunch? We're not safe!"

Brownie frowned for a moment.

"We're not hiding, Keegan. We assess the situation and what we want to do and then make it work. We need to live our lives, Keegan. By hiding, we're letting them win. I won't do that. And I won't let them do that to you. I have a beautiful wife that I want to show the world."

"But, it's only temporary, Brownie. I can't let you put yourself in danger." Keegan was afraid for Brownie. She knew that she loved him, only it was too soon, she thought.

"It's what I do, Keegan. The same for my friends. You're important to me and that makes you important to them."

Brownie found himself the recipient of a sudden hard hug before Keegan just sat with her arm around his neck. He froze for a moment and then smiled. He had not been expecting that reaction from her.

"Brownie? Could this friend find my parents? I would like to know that they are okay and why they left like they did." Keegan was grasping at straws, she knew.

"We can. Just let me have that information and they'll search for them."

Chapter 12

Walker stood where he could watch Brownie and Keegan as they moved through the downtown area that afternoon. He was frustrated that he hadn't been able to take Keegan that morning. She had reacted too quickly. His boss had given him orders. Keegan was to be brought to him and as soon as possible. Baker stood beside him, a slight smirk on his face.

"Not so easy to do, is it?" Baker was still angry that the pair had managed to escape them.

"No, it's not. I still don't understand that. How did they get away?"

"You were too arrogant, you know."

"You didn't think they could or would get away. You need to learn to read people better."

"You could do better? I notice that you sneak around the boss at times."

"As do you." Walker moved away, following Brownie as he stepped into a diner. He walked in and sat down near them, not watching those around him but keeping his eyes on Brownie and Keegan.

Keegan shivered as she felt watched, Brownie's eyes on her. He reached to wrap an arm around her.

"Keegan?"

"Brownie, someone is in here. Someone is watching us."

"I am sure that they are. We expect this." Brownie studied each one that he could see in the diner. He frowned as he could not see everyone's face.

"I know. I just didn't expect it so soon." Keegan stared down at the menu in front of her. "Brownie? How do we do this?"

"Just do what we are. This is a diner that my friends frequent. Those ones from patrol and other officers. They'll look after us." Brownie looked up with a smile and placed their order, his arm around her. He grinned at the looks that they were receiving. It was known in town that he didn't date and here he was with a beautiful lady.

"Brownie?" A voice came from beside him.

Brownie was on his feet, a hand out to shake the man standing beside him before he reached to hug the lady.

"Evan. Flannery. Join us, please. Keegan, my darling, this is Evan and Flannery. We talked about them. In fact, you saw the email from Flannery."

"I did, didn't I? Hi!" Keegan smiled at them. "I hear that you two had an adventure that I needed to talk to you about."

"We did. And I hear that you're in the midst of one." Evan grinned at her even as Flannery elbowed him.

"Don't pay him any mind. He likes to tease at times." Flannery looked up with thanks at the coffee mug placed in front of her. "Thanks, Amy. We'll have our usual."

"Did you two just happen to be here?" Brownie stared between them.

"No, God told us to be here." Flannery nodded at the look that Keegan shot it. "He does that, Keegan."

"I know He does. He did that when we got away from that monster." Keegan looked down for a moment. "I just wish someone had been there to arrest him. Maybe then, we wouldn't still be feeling like we're hunted."

"God's timing is always perfect, Keegan." Evan and Flannery shared a look. "Flannery disappeared on me when we were going through the stuff we did. A good friend and she were kept captive for over a week. They were left to die on an island. It was really hard going through this, but God was there. Each step of the path that we walked, He was there."

Brownie was nodding.

"That He was, Keegan. That He was. Even with our other friends who went through things, He was there." Brownie paused, not quite sure how to proceed. "Evan? Did you get my email?"

"I did and I talked to Jace. He and Emma are tied up on some urgent investigations, but he'll do what he can in the meanwhile. I'll be working on it as well. I talked to Shay. He's already deep into, he said, just from that email you sent him."

"I thought that he would be." Brownie bit into his burger, chewing and swallowing. "Listen, what are you two up to on the weekend?"

"Not too much. Why?"

"I was thinking that we could get together with Shay's, Tag's, and Dougal's. It would do Keegan a lot of good to hear all your stories first hand. Right now, she's feeling overwhelmed and that we're in this on our own. She knows that we're not, but she needs that support." He looked down at her, seeing the shimmer of tears in her eyes. "Is it okay, my darling? Can we do this?"

Keegan nodded, knowing that Brownie had read her right and that she needed to meet with others.

"We can. Our place?"

"How about ours?" Flannery reached to squeeze Keegan's hand. "We're on the lake and can go canoeing or kayaking. It's not too cold for that."

Evan began to laugh.

"But there will be waves and waves are dangerous. Besides you always tell me that the water is cold."

Flannery elbowed her husband once more as she laughed.

"It is. But this time? We need to help Keegan and Brownie forget their troubles for a few hours. Cami and Brett are welcome to join us."

"I'll ask but I think Cami said they had a conference to go to."

Chapter 13

Keegan wandered the shops of the downtown area, not quite sure what she wanted to do. She had thought that she had caught a glimpse of Baker following her but that vision was lost to her as she entered a small bookstore. She was looking for something for herself and also Brownie, but not sure what she wanted.

Flannery had been watching her before she turned to Ayron.

"That's Keegan, Brownie's wife. She's on her own."

"That's Brownie's wife? I see." Ayron moved towards Keegan, the sounds of her footsteps bringing Keegan around in fear. "I'm sorry. I didn't mean to frighten you. You're Keegan?"

"Keegan, this is Tag's wife, Ayron. She's good friends with Brownie." Flannery grinned at her.

"Ayron? Of course. Brownie has mentioned you. Aren't we to do a meal or something this weekend?"

"We are, but we're here now. You're not safe, not yet, are you?" Ayron grinned again as Keegan shook her head. "Okay, so for now, we're your body guards."

"Body guards?" Keegan grinned at the two ladies, causing them to laugh. "What do we do now?"

"You were shopping. Let us stay with you and then follow you home." Ayron frowned as Keegan looked down. "Don't tell me. You walked."

"I did. Brownie took the truck to work. I don't have a vehicle yet. My car has disappeared somewhere, I have no idea where."

"We'll find it for you. Brownie has probably already started on that." Flannery watched around her, finding a man with his eyes on Keegan. Her phone was out and she had taken a picture, sending it on to Evan and also Brownie. "So, Keegan, do you have time for lunch? We would really like that."

"Sure. Yeah. I guess." Keegan was torn, her eyes on a book that she had always wanted to read. "I would really like to get this book but I'm not sure I should be spending the money."

"I have that book. I will lend it to you." Flannery nodded. "I'll give it to you on Saturday."

"Okay." Keegan paused, her eyes on a devotional book. "Just let me pick this up and I'll be with you."

Brownie turned as Keegan approached him later that afternoon. He had been home for a while and was looking for her. He had received Flannery's text and was afraid for her. Baker had been that close to her, and if the two other ladies had not been there, she may well have disappeared.

"Keegan? How was your day?" She walked into his arms and into his hug.

"It was okay. I met up with Flannery and Ayron. Those are quite the ladies." She hugged him back.

"They are." Brownie bit at his lip. "Flannery sent me a text message with a picture."

"She did? Which one?"

"Baker. He was following you this morning."

"That's what they do, don't they? Has anyone said anything about how the investigation is going?" Keegan was hopeful that it was over, and that Brownie could move on with his life. Only, she didn't want that. She didn't want him to walk away from her. Ever.

"No, not really. Justin has been keeping up on it but right now, there's not a lot of evidence. They've been out to the scene of the crime as he worded it, but even there, other than the evidence of the logged trees, there isn't much."

"How did Baker get away? I thought you locked him in the cabin."

"We did. But Walker must have come back. Although Justin said one of the windows was broken out."

"That's what he did then. Broke the window and escaped. Too bad we hadn't been able to do that." Keegan rested her head on Brownie's chest, feeling content, just why she wouldn't say.

—

"We would have been caught if we had tried that. There were also men around."

"I know. Except for that last day." Keegan looked up at Brownie. "I thought we weren't moving until the next day. Why a day early?"

Brownie stared down at her. "I wondered about that." He spun and paced away from her and then back towards her. "Maybe they were alerted that someone had discovered them?"

"Could one of the workers have been undercover?"

Brown nodded. "That's a possibility as well. One of them didn't seem to fit too well. I mean, he didn't stand out or wouldn't to the ordinary eye. But he seemed to be watching the men too closely just to be a fellow criminal."

"And we wouldn't have known that."

Keegan turned to the kitchen counter, intent on fixing their meal.

"I'll grill, Keegan. Do you want chicken?"

"That works. I'll do a salad if that's okay?"

"It is. Keegan, what else happened today?" Brownie stood behind her, his hands reaching to turn her back to him.

"I needed to get some things, and I didn't have much money. I'm sorry to be a burden." She wept even as Brownie hugged her to him.

"No, you are not a burden. Never that. We'll go to the bank tomorrow and I'll get you set up on my

—

accounts. Then you can transfer your money to our bank."

"Okay. I just don't want to draw you down."

"My darling, you never do that. You reach down inside me and see what I can be. I love that about you."

Keegan stood still for a moment, taking in his words. Surely, he didn't mean them. Why would he say that? This was only a sham marriage, one that would last until they had found the two men and their boss. He didn't mean it when he called her his darling. She just knew that.

Chapter 14

Two weeks had gone by. Two long weeks, Keegan decided. They were no closer to finding the men. She had questioned Justin and then the detective who had been assigned to their case, Aaron. He had simply shaken his head. They didn't have enough information yet to even begin to trace the men. She had asked if they were not to be receiving letters, packages, strange emails and text messages. Isn't that what always happened, she had asked him? His grin had grown as she had named all the things that victims usually received. He had agreed with her and told her to just wait. They would surely appear at some time. Keegan had frowned at him and then told him in a grumpy manner that they had better not. What did she do now?

Brownie worried about Keegan while he was on patrol. He had tracked down the youth who had found the body and ensured that he had talked to someone. The youth's parents had been grateful for Brownie's care and compassion. He had walked away, troubled about what had happened. Aaron had not been able to provide much information for him.

Brownie had been back to the site himself, Evan and Tag with him. He had stood, staring around, his memory going back to when he was forced to work there.

"It was here, Brownie?" Evan walked around, studying the area and the stumps that were left.

"It was. Black walnut trees were cut. Black market, for sure. They moved on to another site. I'm just not sure where." Brownie was frustrated. He thought the men would have been caught by now and he could get on with his life with Keegan. Only it wasn't happening.

Tag had been studying the tire marks.

"Someone has been in here recently. Not one of the good guys, as we say." He pointed to the heavy truck tracks.

"There has been." Brownie spun in a circle. "Is there another area close to here that has black walnut trees?"

"Not that I know of." Evan sent off a quick text to Flannery. "Flannery will do some research until I can."

"The cabin? How far was in?" Tag was walking back towards Brownie's truck.

"About a fifteen minute walk. We had nothing in the cabin, other than a wood stove, rough amenities and some worn blankets. No food. No utensils." Brownie was saddened by how Keegan had been treated. "Keegan is healing from that, but she doesn't understand why."

"Did they say what they wanted from her? Besides cooking and cleaning?" Evan was mulling over the possibilities and really didn't like what he was thinking.

"No. That puzzled us. They had to have wanted something, other than that." Brownie pulled up to the cabin and shut off the truck. "I have a good idea what the plan was once we moved. She would never have survived that they planned."

"You are like right." Tag walked towards the house. "The doors are wide open."

"They weren't. Aaron mentioned that they had to have a locksmith come out and open them for the investigation. What is going on?"

Tag stepped inside and stopped.

"Someone has trashed the place. We'll need to call it in, Brownie."

"Yeah, I guess we will." Brownie placed the call. "That's the cabin over there. It looks trashed as well."

"How far did they bring you from the river?" Evan turned that way, hearing the faint sound of water.

"I'm not sure. Keegan isn't either. It can't be that far." Brownie turned as he heard a vehicle and then walked over to Aaron. "Aaron?"

"Brownie? What happened here?" Aaron looked around. "It wasn't like this when we were here earlier."

"I didn't think it was." Brownie turned in a circle. He had not been prepared for this. And he knew that Keegan wouldn't be.

"You didn't go inside?"

"Tag stepped inside and then back out. We were at the cutting area as well. There seems to be fresh tracks from a heavy truck."

"We'll look at that." Aaron was puzzled. "I'm not sure what to think, Brownie. We've looked at your background. Keegan's background. There is nothing there that we can find."

"I didn't think there would be. But there has to be something. Did you ever track down her parents?"

"No yet. Keegan said that they want nothing to do with her. But they hadn't told her why. It's frustrating. We're having to go to their friends and family and they don't want to talk with us. We have spoken with her employer and with her friends. None of them know what happened. Keegan isn't sure about it either."

"No, she isn't. She just knew that her parents walked away from her." Brownie stopped, a thought crossing his mind. "Is she their biological daughter?"

"That we can't determine. Her birth certificate says that she is, but rumours are rife that she is not."

"Okay." Brownie leaned against his truck, arms crossed across his chest. Evan and Tag stood nearby, listening to the conversation. "We need to figure that out. Keegan can't move on totally until we do know."

Evan spoke up.

"Emma and I talked about that. She's running a search and has asked Kataleen to search as well." Micah's wife, Kataleen, one of Abe's security team, had a program that dealt with family trees.

—

75

"That's good." Brownie grinned suddenly. "Aaron, Emma will be sending you lots of information as she finds it. And don't ask how she does. It's her programs that she runs and how her brain works. She can't explain it."

"I've worked with her before. I welcome any aid that she can five." Aaron excused himself for a moment before he returned, a grim look on his face. "Those letters Keegan stated that you weren't getting? One was left here. Though why they did that, I don't understand."

"They knew that we'd come back here at some point. How bad is it?" Brownie was not sure that he even wanted to know.

"Brutal, but I've seen worse. Just stating that they know where she is and that she won't get away from them. Not again. That's a direct threat, Brownie, that they plan to abduct her again."

"We know that they will try. We'll just have to do our best to see it doesn't happen." Brownie shared a look with Aaron. "How many have volunteered?"

"Everyone. You're well respected and liked, Brownie, and this is your hometown. No one wants to see your wife hurt. Or you for that matter."

Chapter 15

Brownie quietly closed the front door behind him that day. He could hear Keegan singing softly to herself somewhere in the house. He stood, back to the door, his head resting against it. Keegan was making his house a home, without trying too hard. He didn't want her to leave ever, but he just didn't want to scare her away. Brownie set his shoes in the closet and then headed for his bedroom, a shower, shave, and clean clothes his intent. He paused, a soft smile crossing his face. Keegan had been ahead of him, laying out his favourite jeans and sweatshirt. Clean towels were in the bathroom. She's spoiling me, he thought. I don't deserve this but she is doing just that.

Keegan turned as she heard the water running and headed for the kitchen, intent on making fresh coffee for them. It was too early for dinner, she thought, as she turned on the oven to bake the casserole she had prepared. She felt arms around her and leaned back on Brownie. She had grown accustomed to his hugs, realizing that he was a hugger, as was his family.

"Have a good day, my darling?" Brownie's voice was soft in her ear.

"I did. Your mom was around and took me out shopping. She can find some awesome bargains."

"That she can. Is it too cold for you to it out back for a while?" Brownie wasn't sure if she would do that for him or not.

"No, the sun is around there and it's warm. The coffee is just made. Supper will be about an hour or so." Keegan apologized for that.

"It's okay, my darling. I don't need to eat when I walk through the door. I never used to, so I don't expect it now." He reached for her hand, drawing her outside and to their favourite seat, a swing. He pulled her down beside him, keeping an arm around her. "This is nice. You've been cleaning out the gardens."

"I have. They were overrun and needed that. Your mom wants to hit the nurseries and garden centres in the spring."

"She loves her gardens. She'll find bargains there as well, I can guarantee you that." Brownie grew silent, content just to it with his bride.

"Something happened today, didn't it?" Keegan was learning to read him.

"It did. Evan, Tag and I headed out to where we were held. Someone has been around."

Keegan nodded, thinking that would have happened.

"They left a note? How bad?"

"Just that you would be back in their control. Aaron was around as the places were trashed. My fellow officers have volunteered to help keep you safe when I can't. But I have a question for you. Evan asked it, actually."

"And that would be?" Keegan waited for Brownie to respond before she turned to him, finding him hesitating to answer. "Brownie?"

"Evan asked if Aaron had determined if you were a biological daughter to your parents."

Keegan looked thoughtful.

"That's something I have always wondered about. Who can we talk to?"

"I know a lady whose husband works for Abe. She uses family trees to research for the police. She'll run a search on you. In fact, she probably has already started it."

"I'm going to owe so many people when this is over. I can't afford all this. It's too much." Keegan was almost in tears at the thought.

"It's okay, my darling. These friends will never charge you a penny. They don't for friends. They understand only too well what it's like to be going through what we are. They have all been there at some point."

Keegan grew quiet, her mind wandering at that thought before she turned to prayer. That was something a former pastor had taught her.

Brownie settled back further, drawing Keegan closer to him. He was worried about her, that was a given. How to keep her safe, that was the question he kept asking himself.

"Brownie? What do I do for employment? Do I find something here?"

"If you wish. There's no rush. Dad was looking for someone to transcribe a devotional book he's writing. Would that interest you?"

"Really? I didn't know that. Sure. I would be but he doesn't need to pay me."

"No, he will. That's not a problem for him or Mom. But do you want to?"

"I'll pray about it. How about in the short term? What are your shifts?"

"I'm off for the next three days. We'll do something fun. We need to."

"Fun? As in?"

"Well, I would like to take you out for dinner. A dress up one. Cami has asked if we could do dinner with them at some point. But I'm not sure what you are interested in?"

"Historical places. Walks in the park. The zoo. You know, stuff you do as kids that I never got to do." Sadness coloured her face.

Brownie simply swept her into a tight hug, his chin resting on her head. *I don't want to ever lose you, my darling. How do we do this? I just know that you'll walk away from me, now or soon, just to keep me safe. And I can't let you do that.*

Hearing the timer from the oven, Keegan sighed. She just didn't want to get up. Brownie made her feel loved and cherished, something that she didn't think she ever had.

"Our meal is ready, Brownie."

—

"I know." Brownie sighed. "I just don't want to get up. I like sitting here with you."

Chapter 16

A week had passed since that night. Keegan had not taken Cameron's offer of employment. Not yet. She simply stated that she wasn't ready to settle to anything. Did he understand? He had simply given her a hug and said he did.

She wandered the house that day, not sure what she wanted to do. Her phone rang, startling her for a moment. Keegan reached for it, turning it to read who was calling. She frowned. A Darcy Foster? Who was she? Then she remembered.

"Hello?" Keegan's voice was hesitant as she spoke.

"Hi? Keegan? This is Darcy Foster. My husband, Doug, knows your husband. Brownie tells me that you two are going through something. Doug and I were wondering if we could pay you two a visit, just to provide some support for you."

"I guess. I can ask Brownie, but I'm sure it's okay." Keegan opened the fridge, staring at what food was in there. "When were you thinking?"

"Tonight. We have to head that way anyway and thought this would be a perfect opportunity to meet with you two."

"Sure. Brownie's not on duty but is out and about this morning." Keegan drew in a deep breath.

"That's fine. We're good anyway you want to meet. Doug has your address. Early afternoon, then?" Darcy could sense the hesitation in Keegan. "Don't worry about a meal. We'll pick up something and bring it with us."

"Thank you. That's not expected."

Darcy laughed. "We're coming to you. We've invited ourselves. It's what we do, Keegan. A friend who has an Irish bakeshop will be delighted to send on some treats. It's how she is. And yes, she and her husband had an adventure as well."

"What is it with you all?" Keegan wasn't really sure what to expect anymore.

"God used us all to bring others to justice. He will do that. We'll see you in a few hours." Darcy hesitated for a moment. "And thank you, Keegan. I know how hard it is to trust anyone at this point."

Brownie stood for a moment, watching Keegan. She still stood with the fridge door open, her phone in her hand at her side. He smiled, not quite sure what was happening.

"Keegan?" He walked towards her as she jumped.

"I didn't hear you." She set her phone down and closed the fridge door. "You're home."

"I am. What's going on?" He was puzzled to say the least.

"Apparently, two of your friends are heading this way. I wasn't expecting anyone. And she told me not to worry about a meal. That they would take care of it." Keegan blinked, not used to that kind of caring.

"They are? Which ones?"

"A Doug and Darcy?" She frowned as Brownie grinned. "This isn't funny, buster."

"No, it's not but that's Doug and Darcy. It's who they are and what they do." Brownie hugged her tighter. "Now, what else have you been up to?"

She shrugged, turning in his arms to face him.

"What were you up to?"

"Just looking around. I had word that a fellow on the street wanted to meet with me. Only he didn't show."

"That's scare me, Brownie. What if it was one of them?"

"That's what Justin and I figured out. He was with me when I went to the meeting place." Brownie bit at his lip for a moment. "We think it was Baker or Walker. Both have been seen here."

"That's strange. Shouldn't they be wherever it is that they are logging next? Or have they moved on from that? And just who is behind them. They don't have the smarts to come up with this on their own. Baker liked his alcohol too much. He was drunk that last day."

"He was. I didn't like how he watched me. It was very unsettling." Keegan leaned against Brownie, hearing his heart beating under her ear.

"It was. I don't want to you fall into his hands again. I don't know what he had planned but it was not for your good." Brownie turned her to face the house. "Now, we need to make some changes here. This is a bachelor pad, not a family home. I would be honoured for you to make into just that."

"But Brownie? This is only temporary, don't you remember?" Keegan was confused.

"That's what we agreed to, my darling. But you see, I have fallen in love with my lady and don't want her to ever leave me." Brownie stared forward, not wanting to see the rejection on her face.

Keegan stared at him in disbelief. Really? That was how he felt. She had thought that, but had doubted her heart. *Is this the path, God, that You have chosen for us? Is Brownie the pathfinder I always dreamed about, who would make my life an adventure with him and with You?*

When Keegan didn't speak, Brownie sighed and turned away, stopping as he felt a gentle hand on his face. He didn't look at Keegan, not daring to.

"Brownie? Is that really how you feel?" Keegan watched with compassion as he hesitated and then nodded. "Oh, Brownie. I didn't know that. I didn't dream that you would ever care for me. I love you too. I just didn't think that you would love me in return."

Brownie had turned as she had spoken, his eyes locking on hers, seeing in hers the love that she felt. He reached to draw her to himself. His dream was coming true, at last. He bent to kiss her and then just held her.

Chapter 17

Three hours later, Darcy Foster watched Keegan, seated beside her on the living room couch. They had been there about thirty minutes, long enough for introductions to be made. Doug and Brownie were in the kitchen, and Darcy could hear the sound of their conversation and laughter. Keegan was uncertain as to what to expect, and it showed. She didn't feel that she had a lot of conversation skills.

"Keegan? It is so good of you to let us drop in on you like this. Newlyweds and all." Darcy grinned at her.

"You are welcome. But I am not sure just why you felt that you had to come." Keegan finally raised her eyes to Darcy.

"I just knew that we had to. Doug is used to me getting these feelings." Darcy reached to squeeze Keegan's hand. "You see, I used to do profiles on criminals. Long story short? I was treated badly by an officer, was in a car accident, and suffered from PTSD. Doug has helped with that. I still do that for friends. We had a really rough time with what we went through. I was targeted by a rogue cop and he killed and injured many people in the towns surrounding ours. So, you see? I do understand to a certain extent what you are facing. I pray that what it is doesn't come close to what Doug and I faced."

Keegan's eyes slid closed. Someone who understood. She knew Brownie's friends and their ladies did.

"Your family? How did they take all this?"

"My family? They have cut all contact off with me. I brought too much trouble to them. I pray that eventually they will reconcile with me. But that is in God's hands and His timing." Darcy shot a glance towards the kitchen. "What can I do for you?"

"Brownie has told you what happened?"

"Emma has. She's worried about you two." Darcy hesitated, then pointed to the folder she had dropped on the table. "This is a profile of who you are facing. I see three different men involved. Doug said a younger man was killed?"

"Yes. Edwin Short. He was someone who had haunted my steps for years." Keegan stared at Brownie as he stood near her. "That's when Brownie was hurt."

Doug nodded. "It's what we hear a lot, Keegan. Even though I am the lead on our emergency task force, I do get involved in events that I can't talk about." He sat nearby, Brownie shifting Keegan over until he could sit beside her.

The four set aside that discussion, rising at last for their meal. When Doug and Darcy left a few hours later, a friendship had been cemented. There were plans for Brownie and Keegan to travel to Riverville to visit them and talk with others of their friends. They just didn't set a time.

—

Keegan cleaned the kitchen and then reached for her sweatshirt. She curled up in the swing and studied the night sky. Today had been overwhelming emotionally for her. Brownie watched her for a while, before he looked down at the folder. He set it aside, instead heading for Keegan, to wrap her in his arms.

The next morning, Brownie stood watching Keegan. He was dressed in his uniform. Keegan was at the kitchen counter, her back to him. She knew that he was there, but she wasn't quite sure how to respond to him. She had avoided him last night, her bedroom door closed early. She needed to think through and pray through their conversation.

"I'm off, my darling." Brownie walked forward, wrapping her into his arms, a kiss on her temple. "I'll be off around three. Would you like to go out for dinner tonight?" He waited until she nodded. "I'll call later. Do you have plans for today?"

Keegan swallowed hard, not sure how to tell him.

"Your mom is coming around. We're going shopping, just for some stuff for the house. You said to."

"Good. Make it your home, Keegan. I'm fine with whatever you do. I didn't do much around here. Other than the basics. Mom and Cami have been after me for years to do that."

"Okay." She turned to face him, searching his eyes and seeing his love for her. "We need to talk,

Brownie, at some point. We need to go over what it was that Darcy brought us."

"We will. I have had emails from Emma and Kataleen that we need to look at as well." Brownie walked away at that point, not sure that he was leaving her at the right point. He had no choice. Duty called, and he just had a feeling it was going to be one of those days.

Keegan turned as she heard her name called. Cara was walking towards her across the lawn. Keegan had stopped to stare at the front of the house, not sure what she wanted to do there, but she didn't like the shrubs. They made her feel unsafe, as if someone could hide behind them and then kidnap her.

"Keegan! You look lost in thought." Cara reached to hug the younger woman.

"I am. It's those shrubs. They're too big. I don't feel safe with them."

Cara stared at her and then at the shrubs before her purse was on the front porch.

"Open the garage, dear. We'll take care of them. I know Brownie has trimmers and saws that we can use."

"But Cara! You're dressed to go shopping! We can't do that!" Keegan was horrified. She listened to the sound of Cara's laughter, not seeing the vehicle that had been parked across the street all morning.

"I'm in jeans and a sweater, Keegan. They will wash. It's not the first time I've done this and I suspect that it won't be the last. Come on. I've talked to Conor about these before and he had agreed

—

that they needed to go. Only, he's not had the time or will to do it. He's told you to make any change that you want?" Cara watched Keegan closely, seeing her eyes close and then the nod.

"He has. Whatever I want to do, he's said to go ahead. But it's his home." Cara moved towards the garage, unlocking the door and then raising it. She searched the tidy, well organized garage for the tools.

Cara headed for what she wanted. This was one way to make Keegan feel a little safer. If they didn't get to shop today, then they didn't. This took precedence.

"It's yours as well. Conor would tell you to go ahead. If he was here, he'd be right here to do it. Now, do you want the saw or the trimmer?"

"The trimmer, I guess, if I can figure out how to run it."

Cara's laughter spilled out. Keegan would bring so much fun to their lives, she thought. This young couple were deeply in love, she knew. How to get them to admit that to one another? That's where God came in. With maybe a little nudge from Mom.

Two hours later, Keegan stood back, an arm around Cara. She was pleased with their work.

"I didn't think that we could do this." Keegan was happy. The front gardens looked bare with the shrubs gone but she knew once spring came, they would fill them all again.

"Of course, we could do it. Cam was glad to come and take the debris away for you. Come spring, we'll hit the garden centres and make this place a

---

showcase of what can be done." She tightened her arm around Keegan. "We didn't get to shop today, but that's okay. I wanted to spend time with my new daughter and did just that."

Keegan froze for a moment before she turned her head, finding Cara watching her, a mom smile on her face.

"Thank you, Cara. I haven't had a mom for years."

"You are so welcome. And here is Cam with food for us. He volunteered to grab a meal when he was out. He's so glad that you are in Conor's life."

Brownie stopped his truck in the driveway, his eyes on the house. It looked different from what it had that morning. His eyes searched the area, feeling eyes on him, and noted the car still parked across the road. He memorized the plate, intending to call it in later. Instead his phone was out and he sent a text in to the patrol officer on duty, who promised to run it right away.

Keegan stood in front of him, uncertainty on her face. Even though she had been told to go ahead with changes, she still wasn't familiar enough with Brownie to judge his reaction.

"Keegan? You've been busy! I like it!" He wrapped her into his arms.

"You do?" She hugged him back, holding on tight. "I wasn't sure. Your mom just took over and we worked away. Your dad took away the debris and then brought us lunch." Tears clogged her throat and clouded her eyes. "I don't remember ever having that with my parents. And I should have."

"You should have. Now, let's get you inside. There's a car across the street that Lou is running the plate on."

Keegan peered around him. "It's been there all day. Your father checked it out, I think, walking up and down the street."

"That he would. Now, let's get inside. I still want to take you out for dinner. We need to be out and about. We're not hiding."

Chapter 18

Brownie stared down at the text message that Lou had sent him. He had seated Keegan at the table in a local restaurant and then sat across from her. This text message was disturbing. He would need to talk to Keegan, but not at the present moment.

"Brownie? Is everything all right?" Keegan's hand reached for Brownie's. "You look worried."

"I am. Lou got back to me about the plate." He looked up at her and smiled. "For now, we'll set it aside and enjoy our evening."

"We can do that. At least, I think we can." Keegan scowled at him as he laughed. "It's not funny."

"No, it's not but you are just so adorable when you look at me like that."

Late that night, Brownie turned from his computer, looking at Keegan as she read back through the information Darcy had given her.

"It says that Walker has a brother. Is that true?" Keegan looked up at Brownie.

"It is. Aaron has proven that and has tracked him down. He wants nothing to do with Walker and hasn't had in years. But he's still on the radar, as they say. So is Baker. He has a sister that we can't track down."

"And she could be involved." Keegan sat back, a frown on her face. "They're not smart enough to do this or to have the resources needed. There has to be someone behind them. That only makes sense."

"It does. Aaron is working that but he doesn't have a lot of information to go from. They are very careful to cover their tracks."

Keegan curled her legs underneath her and reached for a pen and paper.

"But they don't have us. We saw these men everyday. We need to make notes about what we saw, felt, what they said to us, to one another, and to the other men. That's your job, Brownie."

Brownie agreed with her but instead reached for the pen and paper.

"Set it aside for tonight, my darling. It will still be there in the morning. Head off to bed. I'm due in tomorrow for six instead of seven." Brownie hugged her and watched as she walked away, heading for her rest. He wouldn't be sleeping, not that night, he decided. Not that he would be working their case but he would be spending the night in prayer.

Keegan turned the next afternoon, heading for the grocery store from where she had parked in the lot. She felt uneasy, looking over her shoulder frequently. A short time later, she placed the groceries in her trunk and then stood looking around. Spying the bakeshop in the plaza, she nodded. She would find something there for their dessert. It would be as good as what Darcy had brought from her friend's Irish bakeshop, but it would do for now.

Intent on reaching that shop, Keegan headed across the lot, not focusing on the cars around her. She heard a shout and then someone was running towards her. She felt the hot air from the car engine and stumbled as she threw herself sideways. Her head thudded on the asphalt pavement and then all sounds faded. Keegan didn't move from where she lay sprawled on the ground.

Hands reached to assess her and there were calls for paramedics. The patrol officer, Lou, stopped as he saw who it was.

"What happened?" Lou looked around.

"Someone tried to run her down. She wasn't hit but she fell. I think she hit her head. She hasn't moved since she went down." The older man was worried about her.

"Okay. Let me get your statement in a moment." Lou stepped to one side, his hand on his mike. "Dispatch, patch me through to Justin but on another channel."

"Lou?" Justin turned to watch the paramedics work.

"It's Keegan. She was just hurt in the parking lot at the grocery store and bakeshop. We need to get Brownie to the hospital without scaring him too much."

"Okay. I'll track him down. How is she?" Justin moved rapidly through the streets, having an idea where he would find Brownie. He found him at the scene of an accident and just stood on the sidelines until Brownie looked up and waved.

“Justin? You’re here?” Brownie grew pale. “Keegan?”

“Let Adam have your keys to your car. I need to take you to Keegan. She was injured a little while ago.” Justin watched with compassion as Brownie just stood for a moment.

Brownie’s head dropped to his chest even as his eyes closed. Please, Lord, let my lady be okay. I can’t lose her, not yet. Please, Lord? He handed his keys to Adam, feeling his fellow officer touch his shoulder before he was shoved gently towards Justin’s car.

“Justin? What happened?” Brownie stared out the side window, knowing he needed to hear what happened but not certain that he wanted to.

“It looks as if she had been in for groceries and then was heading for another store. A vehicle sped towards her. She managed to evade it but slipped and fell. She’s unconscious, Brownie. Lou was with her. He was going to follow her in.”

“Lou? Okay. He didn’t say how bad Keegan is. He didn’t know.” Justin pulled to a stop near the emergency entrance to the hospital, a hand out to stop Brownie.

Brownie hesitated, a hand on the door handle. He knew Justin hadn’t stopped him just because.

“Brownie, we’re praying for you and Keegan. You know that.” Justin nodded towards the entrance. “We’ll go in and see what they say. Lou was reaching out to your parents.”

"Thanks, Justin. It's just that it's almost too much for us." Brownie didn't continue. He was unable to. How badly was his lady hurt? That scared him.

"We know that, Brownie. We do know that. We're working to try and find these men. Patrols are passing by your place every hour, day and night. They haven't seen that vehicle again. Aaron tells me that Emma and Kataleen are reaching out to him. Darcy has given him the profile that she created of the men. It takes a lot of leg work and investigation to find them and bring them to justice. It is in God's timing, my friend. His and His alone. Why you are walking this path? No one on earth knows."

Chapter 19

Brownie's footsteps sounded on the tiled floor of the hospital corridor. He searched for Keegan, not finding her. The charge nurse hesitated and then came towards him.

"Brownie? You're here?" Becky was puzzled.

"I am. My wife?" Brownie searched Becky's face.

"Your wife? I didn't know that you were married." Becky's frown deepened.

"Keegan. She was brought in after an accident." Brownie could hardly swallow past the huge lump in his throat.

"Keegan? She's your wife?" Becky turned to stare back down the corridor. "She's here but in imaging at the moment. Here. Have a seat in the waiting room. Dr. Peters will be out shortly." Becky watched with compassion as Brownie hesitated and then moved towards that very door.

Brownie sank into a chair, his head going back to rest on the wall behind him, even as his eyes closed in prayer. Justin stood and watched before he sought out Lou.

"Lou?" He studied the other officer for a moment. "What can you tell me?"

"It was deliberate from what the witnesses have said." He grinned. "Some gave chase and blocked him in. He's been arrested and is now downtown. Man by the name of Baker."

"Baker? Him? He's one that we've been looking for." Justin spun. He searched for Brownie, not seeing him. "Now, where did he go?"

"Brownie? He headed back to the exam rooms. Becky came looking for him." Lou waited a moment. "Justin? What is going on? Does anyone even know?"

"That the team is working on. Baker is one of the men who held them captive." Justin sighed. "And it's been a long struggle for those two. Brownie confessed that he is still having headaches at times. That worries me. He didn't get the treatment that he needed at the time."

"No? That is a concern. Listen, I'm off duty. I'll head out and change and come back. He'll need someone with him. His folks?"

"Aaron was heading that way to bring them over. This is hard, you know?" Justin walked away, leaving Lou nodding. They both agreed. This was hard and would only get harder. Even with Baker in custody, it wasn't over.

Brownie stared at Becky as she approached him, rising to his feet.

"Becky? Keegan?" He was worried and scared and it showed.

"Come on back, Brownie. She's in a room right now. Paul thought that he would be around in a few moments. He's just waiting for some results, he said."

Brownie nodded, his eyes on Keegan. He was afraid, he had to admit, that she had been seriously hurt. He didn't know how he would live if he lost her. His hand reached to touch her face, resting against her cheek. Keegan moved restlessly, her head twisting and tossing.

His arm leaning on the side rail, he watched her closely. Brownie didn't turn as he heard footsteps, thinking it was just one of the nurses. He looked up at last to find Paul Watson standing there, his eyes on Keegan's chart.

"Paul?" Brownie's voice was hesitant.

"Brownie? I didn't know that you were married. You've kept it quiet." Paul looked up at that point.

"No, we married very quickly. What can you tell me?" Brownie frowned at the look on Paul's face.

"Brownie? Do you know a medical history for Keegan?" He sighed as he looked back at her chart. "I wondered if you did. No real concerns with the blood work. Now the imaging?" He stopped speaking once more.

"Paul, what is it?"

"She did hit her head when she fell. How serious that is? We won't be able to tell until she wakes up. And that we don't know when will happen. The imaging seems clear from what I see."

"That's good, right?" Brownie's gaze shot between Paul and Keegan, his hand reaching for the one she was using to pluck at the blanket over her.

"It is. She may not remember what happened or she may. That's something we'll address when she awakens." Paul looked around Brownie. "Your father's here."

"Son? What happened?" Cameron was beside Brownie, an arm around his shoulder.

"Keegan was hurt." Brownie blinked rapidly, not willing to let the tears fall. "She's not awaking, Dad."

"She will, son. Justin said one of the officers took her car back to your place. There were groceries in it. Cami headed there to put them away and then is heading this way. Your mom will be here when she's done her meeting."

"Thanks, Dad." Brownie didn't turn to face his father, missing the sorrow that briefly crossed Cameron's face.

"The church is praying for her and for you. Listen, Justin is around. He wanted to speak with you."

Brownie nodded, not wanting to leave his bride, but knowing that he had to speak with his supervisor. Justin stood just outside the room, compassion on his face.

"Brownie? I won't keep you from Keegan for long. I've put you off leave for now. We need to resolve what you're facing. With Keegan hurt, your focus has to be on her."

Brownie nodded, knowing that Justin was correct in his assessment.

"Thanks, Justin. It's what I need to do. I don't think that I've fully recovered from before and now this." He shook his head and then turned to go back to Keegan, standing for a moment watching her and then his father as his father prayed over her.

Chapter 20

Keegan tossed and turned, restless as she tried to sleep, not sure why she felt like she did. Her eyes cracked open and then closed right away. It felt too bright, she thought. She felt a hand on hers and then a hand on her face.

"Keegan? Wake up, my darling?" Brownie bent over the bed, begging Keegan to awaken.

"Where am I?" Keegan raised a hand to rub at her face.

"In the hospital. You were hurt. Can you look at me?" Brownie watched her closely, seeing her drift off to sleep again.

Paul stood on the other side of the bed for a moment, his eyes intent on Keegan before he began an assessment. He stood back at last, his stethoscope around his neck.

"She can go home with you, Brownie. You'll need to wake her every few hours. Bring her back if she isn't any better." Paul handed Brownie the discharge papers. "You are in our prayers, Brownie."

"Thanks, Paul. I appreciate that." Brownie reached to gather Keegan into his arms and walked out of the room, coming to a halt. Now, just how did he get her home? He had no vehicle.

"Brownie?" Cameron stood beside his son, an arm around his shoulders.

"Dad? I need to take Keegan home. Only I have no truck." Brownie blinked rapidly, his emotions raw. He stared down at Keegan's face, seeing the bruising that was starting. He sighed deeply. Just how did he do this, Lord? How did he keep his lady safe? Please, dear Lord, heal her. Bring closure to this.

"That's okay, son. Here, let's get you and Keegan into my car." Cameron looked around as Cara approached, concern on his face. He felt overwhelmed at the moment. This was not what he had expected that day.

"Conor? They're letting Keegan go home?" Cara's hand rested on Keegan's arm, her eyes on her son.

"We're going home, Mom. Only, I don't know how to do this."

Brownie carried Keegan into their home, Cara moving ahead of him to turn down the blankets on the bed. He laid her down, a hand resting on her hair. He blinked rapidly once more, his emotions raw. He could feel the anger starting and prayed to have that relieved and that God would heal his lady.

"It's okay, son. I'll get her settled. You need to get something to eat. Go and get cleaned up, son. I'll get Keegan settled."

Brownie stared down at himself. His mother was right. He was still in his uniform and he had forgotten that. He knelt for a moment beside the bed, his arms around his beloved bride and just stayed still. He couldn't pray but he knew this was when the Spirit would pray for him. That he fully believed.

____

Showered and changed, Brownie took with thanks the mug of coffee his father handed him. He turned back towards the bedroom before his father reached to stop him.

"Your mom's getting Keegan settled. Keegan was awake enough to drink some juice. Here. We'll get some food into you and then you'll be wanting to be with her." Cameron watched his son with compassion, pushing Brownie down into a chair. "We need you to eat this soup, son. Mom pulled it out of the freezer for you."

Brownie finally nodded, his head dropping for a moment. He still was not able to put together a coherent prayer. He was just so worried about his love. He ate what he could and then rose, walking away to find his lady.

His parents stayed for a while, concerned about the young couple. They shared many a look, knowing that Brownie would insist that they leave. Only they wanted to stay but knew that they had to respect his wishes.

Late that evening, Brownie wandered his home. He felt at loose ends, not sure any more what he wanted to do or where he wanted to be, other than where Keegan was. Keegan stood for a moment, wavering as she did so, a hand on the wall to brace herself. She had managed to rise for a while, much to Brownie's consternation. She had even managed to shower and wash her hair, feeling grubby and needing to feel clean.

"Brownie?" Her voice was low and sad. "What happened? I don't remember."

He turned to face her before he was at her side and sweeping her into his arms. He headed for his chair in the living room. Brownie had been prepared for this, his mug of coffee on a table beside the chair along with a bottle of juice, a bottle of water, and Keegan's medications.

"You fell, we think, in the mall parking lot and hit your head. Come, let's sit and then you can tell me what you know." Brownie gathered her close, a blanket tucked over them and under his socked feet.

Keegan cuddled down in his arms. She yawned, a hand going to her face.

"It hurts."

"It will for a while. I have an ice pack here that you'll need to use." Faint humour traced through Brownie's voice at her disgruntled words.

Keegan frowned at him before she sighed, her eyes closing.

"I don't remember much after the grocery store. Did I put everything away?" She was asleep before Brownie could respond.

His head on hers, Brownie prayed. He had no idea where they were heading, either with the investigation or as a couple. He was afraid, more afraid than he had ever been. He too slept, his emotions draining. It had been a busy day to begin with and then having Keegan hurt? That had just worn him out even more. He didn't hear the not so cautious steps that moved around his house. Walker had tracked him down, angry that Baker had been arrested. He blamed this couple. He didn't know that Brownie's security cameras had picked up movement, showing his face in vivid detail as he raised it to study the windows.

Chapter 21

Early in the morning, Keegan roused, not quite awake, snuggling down against Brownie. She felt safe and loved and cherished. She drew a deep breath, wincing as she did so. She felt for her face, finding the soreness, not quite sure what she had done or who she had seemed to have had a fight with. Reaching for the bottle of water, Keegan drank and then set it back, staring at the mug still full of cold coffee and the bottle of juice. She reached for the medication bottle, frowning as she saw her name on it. Why did she have that? Rising at last, Keegan headed for the shower and then stood, her eye on her clothes, dressing finally and then heading for the master bedroom. Brownie hadn't slept there last night, obviously as she had awakened being held in his arms as he slept in his chair. She turned to face the door, a puzzled frown on her face. Just what had happened, she wondered once more. Lord, I am so confused. I have no idea what is going on and I don't like that feeling at all. It seems as if the mystery and adventure surrounding us hasn't left us. Protect my Brownie, please, Lord. Keep him safe as he goes about his daily walk, particularly his job.

Brownie shifted in his chair, not wakening. He would be stiff when he awakened but that was okay. He didn't know that Keegan had stood and watched him before she reached for the mug of coffee and the bottle, heading for the kitchen. She stood for a moment in the doorway, her eye on him, a look in her eyes that she couldn't and wouldn't address.

Rousing at last, Brownie sat up, reaching to fold the blanket. He was puzzled for a moment that he had slept in his chair before his memory returned. He was on his feet, searching for Keegan and not finding her. The aroma of fresh-brewed coffee drew him to the kitchen and he smiled. Keegan must be up, he thought, and reached for the mug that waited on the countertop for him, pouring his coffee and then heading for the back door. Stepping through, he closed his eyes for a moment, drawing in a deep breath of the early morning air.

Keegan looked up startled as she heard the door open and close, her eyes huge for a moment. Brownie sat beside her on the wicker love seat, his coffee mug hitting the table and then just wrapped her in his arms. Keegan tensed for a moment and then sat back, feeling cherished and loved and protected once more.

"Keegan, my darling. How are you feeling this morning?" Brownie dropped a kiss on the top of her head.

"I'm not sure what happened, but the headache is there. Not as bad as it was yesterday." She waited for him to speak. "Brownie? What happened?"

"Baker." Brownie drew in a deep breath, tamping down his anger. "He found you in the mall. You have been to the grocery store and then we think you were heading for another store. Witnesses said that he tried to run you down but you moved and then slipped and fell. You hit your head and knocked yourself out."

"I did? I don't remember." Keegan's brow wrinkled for a moment. "I can remember heading out in the car and then nothing."

"That's normal. Our minds will do that with trauma." Brownie sat for a moment, thinking through what they had been through. "Baker is under arrest, Justin tells me. Aaron will be around today at some point to talk with us. Apparently, he is wanted in many jurisdictions."

"He is? That doesn't surprise me. What about Walker? Has he shown up?"

"Not that I know of, but he may have." Brownie grew silent, content just to sit in silence.

Keegan frowned for a moment. She had thought that she had seen footsteps in the early morning dew.

"Someone has been around, Brownie, during the night."

"They have been? We'll check the video feed in a while."

"Don't you have to be at work?" Keegan knew it was getting close to when he would need to leave.

"I'm not going in for now. I talked to Justin and we decided it wasn't safe. We don't know when I'll be a target and that puts innocent people at risk."

Keegan turned her head to watch his face. Nodding, she simply reached to hug him.

———

"It hurts, I know, Brownie. Let's pray that this is resolved very quickly. Then we can go on with our lives."

Aaron watched Keegan later that morning, not quite sure how to approach her. Brownie watched Aaron in turn, sighing. They were at an impasse, he thought. Baker had refused to talk. They found evidence of Walker moving around the house that morning but he was nowhere to be seen or found. That worried both Brownie and Aaron as if they couldn't find Walker, they could not protect Keegan or Brownie.

"Aaron, what do we do now?" Keegan's voice was quiet. Her face was shuttered and neither man was able to read her.

"We keep searching. Unfortunately, Keegan, we need to set this aside. We'll work on it as we can. Brownie is off work for now, just until we can get a better handle of who and where they are."

"I get that. I just want this over." Keegan's finger rubbed at the tabletop. "I just wish.." Her sentence was unfinished as she was up and away from them. A door closed quietly somewhere in the house.

Brownie's head dropped as he drew a deep breath. This had not gone well, he thought. Keegan would run, he was afraid, just to keep him safe. And that he could not handle.

"Aaron? I know we have to set it aside. I have friends still working on it and I'll make sure that you get all the information that you need."

"I appreciate that, Brownie. I can't emphasize enough that you need to stay safe, both of you.

They've shown that they will come to your home to get at you and take any opportunity that they find. You're being followed, both of you. Any thoughts as to why?"

Brownie shook his head.

"Keegan and I have both wracked our brains trying to figure this out. I appeared to have been at the wrong place when we were taken. We're still trying to figure out why Keegan. Other than that young fellow. He seems to have drawn her in for some reason."

"Interesting character he was. Deep into crime. We have found out that he was related to Baker, a cousin of sorts."

"Related? That's interesting. That's a connection then." Brownie reached for his phone, drawing up his emails. "That's what Evan meant. Let me forward that email to you."

Aaron read the email and then studied Brownie.

"You have interesting friends."

"Evan was an undercover officer and then quit. He lives near here."

"I know. Let me talk with him, then, to see what he says. I can't begin to tell you how sorry we all are that Keegan was hurt, even though we could not prevent it." Aaron looked up to see the devastation that briefly crossed Brownie's face. "I know that you both gave statements. What I would ask if you could write it all out, as much as you can, every little detail that you remember. You know as well as I do that sometimes it's the little details that solve a case."

Brownie turned to watch him, knowing what he was asking.

"I know. I just wish it had been different. Keegan deserved so much more than what she was put through and how we married."

"You love her and she loves you. Sometimes what you go through? That causes you to come to know someone in a deeper way than you would otherwise. And God brought you two together. Don't forget that. He had planned this path for you before you were ever born, Brownie."

Chapter 22

Keegan wandered the yard the next morning. She was at loose ends, used to a routine where she headed out to an office job during the week and then doing whatever she needed to on the weekends. She missed her church family and friends.

Brownie watched her, his head dipping as he sighed. This was dragging on. He had spoken to Justin, wanting to go back on patrol. Instead, he would work in the detachment as a desk officer for the time being. He was trying to be content with that but it was hard, he had to admit. *Lord, help me to be content,* he prayed. *Help those working this to solve this quickly. Keegan needs this and so do I.*

He turned as he heard the doorbell and frowned, glancing down at his watch. They were not expecting anyone, at least he didn't think they were. Opening the door, he stared at the couple, not sure what was going on.

"You are Conor, known as Brownie?" The man spoke in a soft voice.

"I am. And you would be?" Brownie's eyes flickered between the couple.

"I'm Gideon Andrews, Abe's brother-in-law. This is Rebecca, my wife. Emma knew that we were heading this way and asked if we could stop in with information for you." Gideon held up a thick folder.

———

114

"She said that it was too much to email you and she didn't want to courier it."

"I see. She suspects a courier then, I gather? Come on in. The coffee's just ready. Make yourselves at home in the living room and let me find Keegan."

Rebecca grinned.

"Keegan? As in standing behind you?"

Brownie groaned and then reached to pull Keegan to his side.

"I'm sorry, my darling. I didn't hear you."

"No, you didn't. I thought that you were alert? Guess I was wrong."

Brownie ducked the elbow sent his way even as they all laughed.

"Come with me, Rebecca. May I call you that?" Keegan turned for the kitchen. "We have some fresh baking that Cami sent us. Do you drink coffee?"

"We do. Don't go to a lot of trouble for us, though." Rebecca's hand reached to help.

"It's no trouble. I've been bored today and your visit is just perfect, even if it is related to what we're going through."

Rebecca's hand on her arm stilled her movements and brought her eyes up.

"It's okay, Keegan. I understand. I was married before Gideon. What no one knew at the time was that I had a stalker and covered it up, not telling any one. Nick was killed when we had only been married three months. It took Gideon coming into my life to expose who was behind it all. And yes, we did have an adventure that almost killed both of us."

Keegan's eyes grew huge and then she shuddered.

"How did you ever do it, Rebecca? How did you get through it?"

"Support of my brother, Abe, and his team. Support from family and friends. Support from Gideon. We married very quickly to meeting and neither of us regret that, except Gideon would have preferred to court me as he calls it. And most important, God."

"I get that, Rebecca. It is just so hard. I'm trying to find all the verses that I can but I don't have my own Bible and that hurts."

Brownie had stopped just inside the kitchen doorway, his eyes on the women. At Keegan's comment, his eyes slid shut. He had been avoiding that conversation, the one where they needed to go and clean out her place.

Gideon shared a look with Rebecca, shaking his head slightly. This was why they were here, he thought. To help.

"Rebecca, we can help. We really have nowhere that we need to be for the next couple of days."

Rebecca nodded.

"No, we don't. God told us to come and help you. This we can do."

Keegan's mouth opened and closed and then she spun to stare at Brownie, tears glistening in her eyes.

"Gideon is a private investigation, my darling." Brownie moved to draw Keegan close. "He's going to work on our adventure. He and his boss, Sidney, he said. Something seemed familiar about the black walnut trees. Now, what do we do?"

"First, let's pray." Gideon pulled out a chair and sat, his hands reaching for Keegan's and Rebecca's. "God has to go before us. That much we have learned over the years. I grew up with an abusive foster father and lost touch with my sister for ten years because of that. God kept us both as safe as we could be and then resolved that."

Brownie stood for a moment, watching as Keegan cleared the table. Rebecca was helping. Gideon had stepped away for a moment, not letting Brownie know that he was sending out a group text to his friends and what friends of Brownie's that he knew, with Keegan's address. He stepped back into the house, meeting Rebecca walking towards him.

"Rebel?" Gideon swept her close, his eyes pointed towards the kitchen.

"This is so hard, Gideon. Every one who goes through this has added to our lives. But Keegan is different and I don't know why. She is troubled and alone. Maybe that's it?"

"It could be. I asked Sidney and Emma to start a search on her and her parents. For them to walk away like that? It just doesn't seem right, but I know that it does happen. It happened to Darcy."

"I know. She has her moments when she grieves for that lost relationship."

Chapter 23

Brownie reached for Keegan's hand as he stared at the small apartment building. Four units, she said, with her unit on the bottom left. He was afraid suddenly, not sure what they faced.

"Keegan? Do you have a lot of things?"

"Not really. It was furnished so I only have personal stuff." She looked around as she heard footsteps. "Brownie? What's going on?"

"Gideon called some friends. They are here to help." Brownie introduced her to those that she didn't know. "We'll make quick work of this. Now, the landlord?"

"Landlady. She lives next door in that house." Keegan headed that way, Brownie heading with her. Her keys to the apartment had been handed to Gideon, who watched Keegan before he turned to the others.

Keegan walked down the sidewalk and to the other house, hesitating for a moment as tears clouded her vision. She felt Brownie's arms around and then heard the house door opening.

"Keegan, dear? Where have you been? I have been so worried." Her landlady stood on the porch, watching, her arms wrapped in a shawl draped around herself.

"Mrs. Jean, I'm sorry. I didn't mean to be gone so long. I meant to phone you but just didn't. I'm so sorry." Keegan ran towards her and into her hug.

Jean hugged her back, before she set her back, her hands reaching for Keegan's.

"I was so worried about you. It's been so long since I saw you." She looked up at Brownie who had come to stand right behind Keegan. "And this is your young man." She reached to hug Brownie, surprising him.

"I am, ma'am. Keegan and I were married a few weeks ago. I didn't know that she still had an apartment until today. We've had so much going on."

"You have? Keegan?" Jean turned to her.

"We were kidnapped, Mrs. Jean, for a month. Then all sorts of things have been happening. Has anyone been around here?"

"To tell you the truth? No." Jean frowned for a moment. "No, that's not true. There was a man who came to the apartments, looking for you. Said he was your brother. Only we know that you don't have a brother. I have pictures of him. Come in and I'll hand them to you." Jean led the way into her home and was back in just seconds. "Here."

Brownie reached for them, a dark look briefly crossing his face.

"We know him. He's one of our abductors."

"He is? And he was here looking for you. But what could he want?"

"When were these taken?" Keegan looked at them. "Oh, wonderful. They are time stamped. Brownie, this is during those four weeks."

"It is. So they knew all along where you lived." He blew out a breath of frustration.

Jean studied the young couple.

"No one has been back around. But that's not why you're here, is it, Keegan?"

"No, it's not. I'm giving up the apartment, Mrs. Jean. My home is with Brownie now."

"I know it is, dear. It's only right. That's okay. You've paid me up to the end of last month. I won't take another dime from you for it. Have your friends come over when they're finished packing you up. I'll have a meal ready for you all."

Brownie's mouth opened and closed.

"There are a number of us."

Jean grinned, suddenly looking like her young granddaughter.

"I know, but I used to have a catering business. I'll manage." She grew sober. "You know, that man in the photo? He used to hire my company for business meetings."

"He did? Then can you provide any information on who would have been meeting with him?"

"I most certainly can. Let me have your email address, young man, and I will send it off to you today."

———

"That's great. And here it is. I also included the address for a friend who does investigations and also the investigator on my force."

Jean thanked him, a thoughtful look on her face as she read the names. So Emma was involved. This is wonderful, she thought. Dear sweet Emma. She had helped Jean out a few years ago, solving a problem that she had had, taking nothing in return for it, just asking that Jean pay forward that debt. And this was the way she would, by helping her sweet friend, Keegan.

Gideon stood on the sidewalk, watching the couple walk back towards him. He was troubled. There was evidence that someone had been in the apartment over the last couple of weeks. He had made the call to the police and patrol officers were on their way. This would slow down the packing. His friends milled around as did Brownie's. Evan stood beside him, Tag and Shay as well.

"This goes a lot deeper than just what they think." Evan's voice finally broke the silence.

"I know it does. And that worries me. I've seen too much of this with friends and family." Gideon hesitated to speak, catching Brownie's thoughtful look.

"Gideon? Someone's been inside?" Brownie's question caught at Keegan's attention and she looked between the men.

"We know that Walker was around when we were held captive. My landlady has photos of that. She also knows him from when she had her catering business. She's digging up information and emailing it to us." Keegan stared towards the house. "I guess that means we don't go in quite yet."

"Not yet, my darling." Brownie's arm was around her. "We wait for the patrol officers to go through and then we walk you through. People, Mrs. Jean has asked us for a meal when we finished. With all of us here, it shouldn't take long to pack up Keegan. Let's break off into groups and spend some time in prayer. We are going to need it, that much I know."

Chapter 24

Later that day, Keegan stood in her apartment, staring around. Her things had been packed up, the house cleaned by the ladies and she was ready to head over to Jean's for the meal that was promised. Flannery and Ayron approached her, Breckon and Rebecca already beside her.

"This is a new chapter for you, Keegan. We've been through something similar, so we understand to a certain extent what you are feeling. Not that we can truly understand as each circumstance is different." Breckon bit at her lip for a moment. "But God knows. He has already walked this path before you. He has prepared you and Brownie for this. Brownie is a dear friend, and you are just so right for him. We treasure his friendship. Ayron grew up with him so she knows him the best of us all."

"You did?" Keegan turned to Ayron. "Thank you. He treasures his friends and looks out for them."

"He does. And that now reflects back on you, our friendship with him." Ayron looked around. "We all live close to one another. How be we ladies meet and see what we can figure out about this? Rebecca, we'll bring you in on a conference call."

Rebecca began to laugh, bringing questioning eyes to her.

"We can do that. And I can guarantee that my friends and Abe's team's ladies will want to be involved. Let's set up something now. How about two days from now, mid-afternoon?"

"That works." Keegan reached to hug the ladies and then led them from the apartment, shutting the door to it and to a chapter now closed in her life.

Brownie moved through the house later that evening, seeing that Keegan had unpacked her things and made room for them. He smiled as he reached for a picture of the two of them from today. He didn't know who had taken it but it caught them looking at one another. He could see the love showing in her eyes and knew that it was in his.

Keegan watched him for a moment before she moved into his space, reaching to wrap arms around him.

"Thank you, Brownie."

He simply smiled and kissed her.

"You've gotten everything unpacked?"

"Most of it. There are still some things I am not sure that I want to keep. I set those boxes in the garage."

"That's good."

"Listen, we need to go over that material that Mrs. Jean gave us."

"Tomorrow, my darling. Right now, I just want to sit and cuddle with you." He grinned at her. "I have a feeling that things are going to get a lot harder for us and we need to spend this time just in prayer and with one another."

The next morning, bright and early, almost before it was dawn, Brownie was on his feet. He stood for a moment by the bed, watching Keegan as she still slept. He was suddenly afraid for her, knowing that their adventure was not over, not by a long shot.

Moving to his home office, he reached for the paperwork that Jean had given them. His head bowed for a moment before Brownie opened the envelope. He felt fear as he did so but continued, his heart raised in prayer. He sorted through the documentation, and then gathered it all up, heading for his dining room table where he could spread it all out and sort it that way.

Heading for the kitchen, Brownie paused as a thought crossed his mind. He shook his head. There was no way someone that prominent in town would be involved, but then he paused again in his forward walk. He knew better than that. He had seen it too many times.

Keegan stood beside the table, her finger moving the paperwork around. She recognized a number of names and then reached for a single piece of paper. This is who it is, isn't it, Lord? She felt Brownie's arm around her even as he handed her a mug of coffee.

"Who is that?" Brownie set his mug down and then reached for the paper. A sigh rose from him. "He's who I think it is as well. He's prominent in this town."

"I know. I'm afraid of him. How do we protect you?"

"I don't know. He'll go after you as well. What did I ever do to him to cause this?" Keegan twisted in his arms, her arms wrapped around him as she sobbed. It had all become too much for her.

Brownie tightened his arms around his beloved Keegan, swaying slightly to try and comfort her. He had no idea what they were to do. Abe had been in contact the day before, after speaking with Gideon, talking him through different scenarios and what they could and could not face. Brownie knew that Keegan would be on her own when he was at work and just wouldn't stay home. Not that staying home would keep her any safer. Walker had been around their place. Abe had promised to send Joseph, his security systems expert to see them and upgrade their system. That he appreciated, but he had a good system already.

"Brownie? When we go through this information, can we set up a database or something? I think we'll find a lot of connections to Walker and Davis."

"I think we will. Jean emailed me again. Walker has been around the property again. She called the patrol officer but Walker was gone by the time he got there. They're looking for him for trespassing at the very least. His fingerprints were in your apartment."

"They were?" Keegan turned back to the table, a finger tapping at her lips. "Could he have planted something that I brought with me?"

"Tag thought of that. Ayron mentioned something in passing and that triggered him. They searched everything as it was packed. So, no, we didn't bring anything with us."

Three hours later, Brownie sat back. Keegan had drawn up a computer program of sorts but was not quite satisfied with that. He looked around, wondering who he could talk to and then reached for his phone as it chimed. Micah, from Abe's team?

"Micah? How are you and Kat?" Brownie moved away, standing in the hallway where he could watch Keegan.

"Brownie? We're fine. But how are you two? Gideon was talking to Kat and me last night. We would like to meet with you two. Is that possible?"

"It is. We have been working on setting up a database but we need some help on that."

"Well, we're in your town right now. Is this a good time?"

"It is. Here's our address."

Keegan looked around at that.

"Brownie?"

"It's Micah. He's Abe computer expert and can help us with our program."

"Okay, that will help." Keegan was on her feet, moving to the kitchen. "It's almost lunchtime. We need to feed them."

Brownie was at the door, greeting Micah and Kat and then staring at the bags they held.

"We brought lunch, Brownie. It's just salads, sandwiches and fruit. I hope that's okay."

"It's more than okay." Keegan peeked around Brownie. "I'm Keegan. Come on through to the kitchen. The dining room table is buried right now."

Micah grinned. "Buried is it? Any paper on the walls yet?"

Keegan stared at him and then laughed.

"No, but we can. Is that what you suggest?"

Chapter 25

Micah stood late that afternoon, deep in discussion with Brownie. Aaron had shown up earlier and was in conversation with Kat and Keegan. He hadn't realized that Kat was the one who had sent him the information on the family trees. This was her business, using family trees to track criminals. She had almost lost her life over that program.

"I think this should be what you need, Aaron." Kat handed over a sheaf of papers. "We've worked what we can with what Keegan and Brownie have amassed. I tend to agree with their assessment as to who it is."

"And that would be?" Aaron looked over at Keegan. "Keegan?" When she named the person, he paled. "You're sure on that?"

"I think so. Brownie feels the same." Keegan looked around for Brownie. "Talk to him."

"I will. I'll look this over and be in touch. It will help. Thank you. Now, what do we do with you?" Aaron grinned at her.

"I have no idea. I'm tired of staying home. I need to do something and I don't know what."

"I see. Tell you what. I'll see what I can do for you."

"Thank you, but you're busy. Too busy, I suspect. I'll manage." She watched as Aaron walked away. "It's true, Kat."

"You feel caged, uncertain of your relationship with Brownie, even though you two are in love. You're used to working and can't."

"That's it. So, what do I do?"

"Are there college courses that you want to take and haven't been able to? How about writing? Ever thought of that? What else?"

Keegan stared at her.

"How did you do that? Come up with those suggestions?"

"Because it's what we've done as ladies. I need to bring them all here to meet you. Only there are so many of us."

Keegan continued to stare at her.

"How many?"

Kat shrugged, a grin on her face.

"A dozen or more?"

Keegan's mouth opened and closed a few times. Her eyes were huge.

"That many?"

"Yep. And we all survived. God protected us, not quite in the way that we expected."

Micah's arm slid around his wife.

"Telling tales, Kat?"

"I am. I need to bring the ladies over here to meet with Keegan."

"How be we head your way later in the week?" Brownie grinned at Keegan. "We can do that."

"That works. We'll set up a date then." Micah moved towards the door.

"Thank you for coming by. This will help us." Brownie locked the door after them and stood for a moment with his hand on the door. *Where do we go from here, Lord? I can't keep my love safe and that scares me more than anything.*

Keegan watched him. Her prayer was for her groom, knowing how troubled and conflicted he was and that she just couldn't help him. She turned back to the dining room, tidying up their piles of material, and then just sitting in front of the laptop. Brownie had set up her computer but for now, the laptop was what she needed. She started a search of her parents, not finding out much. She had had a long talk with Kat that day and Kat had promised to look into it for her. Keegan had been grateful. This was a path that she had walked for years, not knowing why it had happened. Her parents had never said.

Brownie knelt beside her, his arms around her, his chin on her shoulder.

"Looking for something, my darling?"

"I am. I am looking for Mom and Dad. They never said, you know, why they left. I think that I begged them to in my mind, wept in my sleep, and they just turned their backs without contacting me. I need to know. Just for closure." Her head turned, finding herself almost nose to nose with him.

Brownie could see the tears in her eyes and hugged her tighter.

"I know, my darling. It affects who you think you are and how you think that you are perceived. Kat will do what she can. I know Emma was working on that, just as she always does. She looks into anyone and everyone that we are connected to. They won't leave anything uncovered or any stone unturned. Aaron was grateful to get what he needed."

"He was. He asked me about the apartment and that. He had asked briefly before but today he went into great depth with it. He thinks that Walker and Baker had been following me for a while."

"I think that they were. As to why, I don't know." Brownie's hand reached for the mouse and he clicked on an article. "This is interesting. Are these your parents?"

"They are." Keegan read it and then paled. "That's my parents the reporter is talking about. And Walker. How are they connected?"

Brownie printed the article and then sent the link to Aaron, Kat and Emma.

"I'll let them look into it. We'll set it aside for today. Tomorrow, Mom has asked if we can come for dinner. I said I would ask you."

Keegan leaned against him.

"I would like that. Your mom is just so special and loving. So are your dad and Cami."

"Okay. I send her a text later that we can. But what do you want to do tomorrow?"

Keegan shrugged. She really had no idea.

"Your gardens, Brownie. Do you have any spring flowers?" Her eyes were steady on him.

"No, not that I know of. I've just kind of left the shrubs, which you rightly trimmed and removed. That's what we can do. We can find the flowers that you want and plant them. We'll hit all the nurseries, home improvement and department stores, and buy a lot. That will keep Walker or whoever it is trailing us busy." He grinned as she shook a finger at him. "Have I told you today that I love you?" Brownie simply reached to kiss her.

Chapter 26

Walker was frustrated. He had spent the day following Keegan and Brownie, wandering through garden centres and department stores, not close enough to listen to their conversation but forced to watch from a distance. He missed Baker at this point. They could have traded off.

He needed to find someone else, Walker decided, but who, that was the question. He turned, heading for his apartment and his notes. There had to be someone that he knew.

Reaching out to his employer, he didn't like the response. It was dropped back on him. Walker had been bluntly told that this was his problem and he had to solve it.

He grew angry. His anger swelled against Keegan. She was not to have escaped from him. Brownie was incidental to it all. He ruffled through the papers and found a name. Yes, he thought, this person would do. She would pay and pay dearly for that. She had forced them to move onto a new site before they were finished with the last one.

Walker headed for a bar downtown where he knew the man he searched for would be. He sat, a drink on the bar in front of him, watching for his contact. It didn't take long for that woman to appear. She slipped to a seat beside him, not looking directly at him.

———

Waiting quietly, Walker sipped at his drink. The envelope that he had laid in front of him was slid carefully along the counter to the woman. She waited and then picked it up, sliding it in turn into her handbag. Without a word, she was up and gone. As she passed a darkened doorway, the letter was slipped into the hands of the man who stood waiting for her. The woman was gone almost before he had it in hand.

The man stepped from the doorway, looking around as he tucked the letter into a pocket and then walked back towards the bar. He slipped inside and just stood, his eyes watering from the smoke and his stomach roiling from the smell of alcohol. Nodding, he walked away. He would play his part, that he knew.

Justin looked up from where he sat at a diner in the downtown area. He frequented one that had been a favourite of his when he was a street cop. He knew the people of the area, that they would help. Or most of them would. He didn't look up as a man slid into place across from him.

"Justin? Here. He's looking for an assassin." The envelope was dropped on the table and the man was gone.

Justine didn't acknowledge that he had been there, simply dropping his menu on the envelope. Anyone who knew Justin knew he didn't need to read the menu. He looked up with a word of thanks as a plate of bacon and eggs and toast was placed in front of him, moving the menu towards him and tucking the letter into his pocket. He didn't think he had been seen but he knew that people were looking out for Brownie and his lady.

———

Back in the office, Justin sat at his desk, pulling out the letter, placing it on the blotter o his desk. He just sat and stared at it. When he opened it, he knew it would change what they were looking at and investigating. Walker was hiding but he knew where he was. It was the people that Walker had hired he was worried about. They didn't know who all those were.

He looked around as Aaron paused at his doorway and beckoned him in. Aaron entered, closing the door at Justin's request before he sat across from him.

"Justin? I was looking for you but you look puzzled."

"I am, Aaron. Someone handed me this letter. It comes from Walker apparently. I haven't opened it yet. Susie is on her way to test it for us." Justin looked up, nodding. "I would say that he's upping his game."

"We thought that he would. How do we keep those two safe?"

"That's the question. Keegan cornered me the other day, asking why they weren't getting the normal stuff as she calls it." He grinned for a moment as he recalled the furious look on her face.

"She did, did she? I'm surprised that they're not. Brownie mentioned that there has been movement on their security cameras but whoever it is keeps his face hidden."

"Or her face."

"True. I've seen the stills that he's printed off. It could be a woman as well." Aaron watched as the door opened at Justin's request and Suzie entered.

"Here, Suzie. Check this out please and then bring it right back. It involves Brownie and Keegan."

Suzie's eyes shot to him and then she nodded. She was away and then back in short order.

"I found some prints and will run them. The letter is about what you would expect."

Justin reached for the evidence bags and then at Aaron.

"I guess we find out, don't we, what Walker wants." He read the letter and then handed the bag to Aaron. "He's looking for an assassin."

"That's what we thought. They got away and now must pay. Only we don't have the manpower to keep with them."

"No, and Brownie wouldn't accept it, even if we did. We'll need to talk with him and Keegan."

Aaron sat back, his eyes on the letter. It simply stated that Walker knew the man was an assassin for hire. He wanted to hire him to take out a couple. Walker would be waiting for the man to contact him, by leaving an ad in the local newspaper.

"He's playing it cautious. It's not the first time that he has done this. That much is obvious." Aaron laid the letter back on the desk. "I'll go talk with him. He's on duty tomorrow, is he?"

Justin nodded, a frown momentarily crossing his face.

———

"He's here in the detachment. Not happy but he understands." Justin sighed. "This is going nowhere fast."

"I know. We're missing one simple fact. Brownie said that a friend's wife was working on a family tree for the two abductors. She'll forward it as soon as she can."

"Kat?" At Aaron's nod, Justin leaned forward. "That's good. I've seen her work. She is thorough. I would suspect that her husband is working on it as well."

"He is. They were around the other day, Brownie said. Emma's working it as is her brother-in-law."

"Good. Emma can find information like no one else. A friend or two of Brownie's work for her."

"They do?" Justin was surprised, having forgotten that he had been told that.

"Evan and I believe Shay." Aaron rose, fatigue hitting for a moment. For some reason, they were swamped with cases. "You know, all of a sudden we are swamped. I wonder if Walker is doing this to keep us from investigating Brownie's case." He looked up at a sound from Justin.

"I think that you are right. The cases seemed to increase about the time that Brownie disappeared. That young fellow? How far did you get with him?"

"Not too far. No one wants to talk about him. And that is strange. Someone is stoking fear among his friends and cohorts."

———

"I think that you are correct. And I would like to know who."

Justin spoke a name, bringing a shocked look to Aaron's face.

Aaron nodded. "I think that you are correct. They would have the means to transport the logs and the contacts. I'll do some digging." He paused as his phone chimed and he pulled up an email. He gave a quick grin. "Evan is ahead of us. He has already pinpointed that name and is working on it."

"He's good. The force he was on lost a good officer when he retired."

"It did, but he was burnt out. He needed a complete break." Aaron walked away, his thoughts already on what he could do to find the people.

Chapter 27

Brownie was at a loss. He enjoyed working the streets, they had his heart, and to be unable to? He felt like a part of himself was missing. Knowing why it was necessary still didn't ease the heartache that he felt. Keegan had watched him that morning before simply moving in to hug him. Her whispered prayer in his ear had helped to some extent.

Keegan had watched Brownie walk away to his truck, a hand on the door before she closed and locked it. Still a prisoner, she thought, only the surroundings are a lot more comfortable. She sighed, a deep from the toes sigh. What did she do with her day? She had cleaned and cleaned until the house was sparkling. She couldn't bake, she had already done that. The meal for tonight, a casserole, waited in the fridge.

Pulling out her phone, Keegan hesitated before she dialed a number

"Hello?" Ayron's voice echoed across the line.

"Ayron? It's Keegan. I'm sorry. I should not have called you. You're likely at work." Keegan's finger moved to cut the call.

"No, actually, I'm not. I only work part time and today is my day off. You're feeling caged and wanting to be out and about. Breckon and Flannery mentioned that to me last night. We are suggesting that we have a girls' day out. Are you in?"

"A girls' day out? Oh, I would be. Where?"

"Well, we could go shopping and out for a meal. Or we can gather at one of our places. Flannery wants you to come visit her."

"I would like that. I miss the friends from my hometown. I don't know who I can trust from there, though."

"That's what Tag and I were talking about. He said he'd talk to Brownie and get a list of your friends. Now, are you ready to have some fun?" Laughter sparkled across to Keegan.

"That I am. Brownie's working in the detachment and would be done by three."

"Not a problem. Our guys will meet us wherever it is we end up. Oh, and Dougal and his wife. McKala, are in town as well. Dougal is with Evan, Tag, and Shay. McKala is here with me."

"That sounds wonderful. I'll meet you somewhere."

"No, I'm standing at your front door right now." Ayron tucked her phone into a pocket. "Come on, Keegan. Let's party!"

Keegan stared at her and then moved back.

"Come in for a moment. Where's McKala?"

"Right here. I am so glad to meet you." McKala simply reached to hug Keegan.

"And you." Keegan looked uncertainly at her clothes. "I'm not sure that I am dressed correctly." She studied what the others were wearing.

———

"You are dressed just fine. Just grab a sweatshirt or jacket, your purse, and your phone."

Keegan sat back late in the afternoon in a chair in Ayron's living room. Her face was flushed with laughter. What a wonderful group of ladies, she thought. I missed having friends like this.

Brownie stood for a moment in the hallway, watching her. Tag's hand rested on his shoulder.

"Looks as if our ladies are getting along quite well. Keegan needs that."

"She does. She hasn't said much about her friends from before, but I got the impression that she didn't have many and that they were not really close. She seems to have spent a lot of time alone."

"Our ladies will change that." Dougal watched Brownie closely. "We're not right here in town but we're not that far away. And I know Holly and Lincoln would be open to meeting her." Dougal mentioned a lifelong friend of his and her husband.

"Thanks, guys. Now, do we eat here or not?"

Tag laughed as he moved towards the kitchen and where Ayron was peeking around the door frame, simply wrapping her into a hug. He dropped a kiss on her forehead.

"Thanks, love. She needed this."

"She did. She is so sweet. She and Brownie are just so well suited. God did good again." She smirked as Tag laughed at her. "There is chicken, ribs, and hamburgs ready for the grill. Breckon and Flannery brought salads and dessert."

"This is wonderful." Brownie reached to hug Ayron before moving towards his wife. Keegan had not heard or seen the men entering, giving a small squeak as Brownie simply wrapped her in his arms and moved her over enough that he could sit before he pulled her down onto his knee. "Have a good day, my darling?"

Keegan's face still sparkled with the enjoyment and fun from her day.

"I did. These are such wonderful friends. I missed out in life by not knowing them sooner."

Evan grinned as he sat beside Flannery.

"They are fun ladies to know, Keegan. And I can guarantee that you'll likely tire of them." He laughed as Flannery elbowed him.

"Not likely. They have also offered to help solve our mystery, Brownie. Isn't that great?"

"Very great. Now, we have so many working on it, it should be solved in no time." He sobered for a moment, thinking of what Justin had approached him about. He needed to speak with Keegan about that but now was not the time.

Shay nodded to himself as he watched Brownie. Something has come up and it is hard for him to set it aside. He made a note to himself to speak with Brownie.

Late that night, Keegan stood in the living room, looking lost for a moment. Brownie watched and then moved in to simply hold her.

"Keegan?"

"Brownie? How long will this take? I want it over yesterday. Who else do we need to look at?"

"Right now, the investigators are looking at everything, running down leads, confirming information, talking to witnesses and informants. It is frustrating, I know, but this is how it works. We have to let them, even as we work through things ourselves. Listen, Justin talked to me today. Walker is looking to hire an assassin. He received a letter to that effect."

"Of course he would. Isn't that what they do? Take out witnesses and their victims. How do we stay safe?"

"That's a worry. I'm safe at work, just not going back and forth and when I'm at home. You, on the other hand, are at risk all the time. I don't know how we do this. All we can do is pray for God to protect you. He knows the path that we are walking, even though we feel lost on it and the way seems dark."

"How do you do this, Brownie? How do you calm me with those words?"

Chapter 28

Hitting his front door on the run, Brownie fumbled with his keys, dropping them a number of times before he could insert the right one and twist it to unlock the door. The door flew open even as he flew through it. He searched, not finding Keegan at first glance. His heart fell. She was gone.

Justin had followed Brownie as he drove rapidly to his home, standing on the porch, searching for Keegan.

"Brownie?"

"She's not in the house. I don't have any hiding spots that she could find. He's got her!"

"Not necessarily. Would she have gone somewhere?" Justin stepped back off the porch, looking towards the houses surrounding him.

"She might, but I don't know that she would." Brownie's hands ran through his hair. His phone rang at that moment and he pulled it out, fear on his face. "Keegan?"

"Brownie? Where are you?" He could hear the fear in her voice.

"I'm at home. Where are you?"

"With Breckon! She came by just a bit ago and pulled me out of the house. She made her go with me. Why?"

"Someone tried to break in. I got the alert and came home. I couldn't find you." Brownie choked back the sobs of fear and worry that choked him. "Are you okay?" He turned as he heard running footsteps, Justin's hand on his back to brace him as Keegan's body hit him hard. Brownie simply hugged her tight and then swept her into his arms, carrying her to his truck.

Watching as Brownie stood beside his truck, not letting go of his bride, Justin shook his head. He turned as a patrol officer approached and had a quiet word with him. Things were escalating with these two and he was at a loss as to how to keep them safe. Today proved that Walker would go to great lengths to take Keegan once more.

Brownie looked around, seeing Breckon standing nearby, worry on her face.

"Thank you, Breckon. How did you know?"

Breckon shrugged.

"Dad came across something and sent me this way. I arrived, Keegan was unsettled, and God told me to take her out of the house." Breckon's father was an investigator. "It looks as if my feelings were correct"

"They were. Walker was around, trying to break in. But he was gone by the time we got here." Brownie turned to watch his house. "Did he make it in?"

"Not that we can tell. The security system worked." Justin stood beside Brownie. "We need to do something with you two. They'll keep trying and someone will get hurt if they come to see what is going on."

"I know." Brownie blew out a breath of frustration. "Where do we do?"

"Put you away somewhere. And that has to be away from here." Justin turned as Aaron approached. "Aaron?"

"Brownie. Keegan. It's time to move you somewhere."

Keegan stared at him and then at Breckon, finding her watching her. A slight smile was on Breckon's face. She knew what Keegan's response would be. It was the same one that she had had.

"I'm not going anywhere. This is my home and I refuse to let him chase me from it. That's what he wants. To get us somewhere we don't know the area or the people around us. Here we do. He didn't make it through the security system, now did he?"

Brownie rubbed at his upper lip, trying to hide the grin that was appearing. He agreed with his bride.

"She's right, guys. Here is where we make our stand. And make a stand we will. Abe and his team will be here tomorrow to help set up for this coming battle."

"They will?" Justin and Aaron shared a look. "Well, okay then. He's topnotch in the security field."

The men finally left, Breckon moving close to Keegan as she watched Brownie walk towards the house. Keegan was afraid, more afraid than she had

---

ever been. She turned to Breckon, opened her mouth to speak, and then snapped it closed.

Breckon's arm was around Keegan as she turned her back to the house and followed Brownie.

"We'll make plans, Keegan. It's what we do. Abe will have good ideas for you, that much I know."

Brownie wandered his house later that night. Keegan had finally headed for bed, not sure of what to say or do. Brownie felt the same way. He could feel the danger building, knew that Walker wanted them dead, but he had no idea who would be the one chosen for that deed. He feared for his bride and for his family. He knew that they would go after them to get to Keegan and himself.

Brownie slumped into his favourite chair in the living room, his thoughts gloomy. Once more, he could not form the words that he needed. All he knew was that he was walking a path that he had never walked before and really didn't want to but he had no choice.

Chapter 29

A week later, Brownie walked his backyard. There had been no further incidents, which concerned him. Keegan had simply looked at him that morning and turned and walked away. There was nothing that they could say to one another. Aaron had no new update. Justin was just watching closely, seeing the strain and stress starting to show in his officer's face.

Abe had been around, making suggestions, having his security system upgraded. Emma had been in touch, but had to set aside what she was investigation for him in order to handle the urgent requests that she had received. They understood that, Brownie and Keegan had said.

His friends were working for them, trying to keep them upbeat and confident that they would find Walker and whoever it was that he had hired. That was the unknown.

Keegan stopped beside Brownie, reaching to wrap an arm around his.

"What do we do, Brownie? We can't hide. It's not fair to you to have to do so."

"Nor you. We'll figure it out. Now, today, we need to do something fun. We've been keeping ourselves in the house, trying to make sense of everything. We need to step back and let it brew for a bit, as Mom would describe making a cup of tea."

"We do. What do we do?" Keegan leaned against Brownie, still in awe of his height and strength. He was the epitome of who she had dreamed about. Only she never thought she would find someone like him.

"Well, lunch out for one thing. Then, we can wander the stores downtown if that's what you want."

"That's not much fun for you."

"It is. I might find something for you. I intend to bring you gifts and flowers and whatever it takes to court you. You missed out on that." Brownie turned her to the house, locking up after them and then heading for the downtown area.

Keegan paused in a small gift shop, her eyes on the small hand-blown glass angels. Her fingers lightly traced one before Brownie had it in his hand, ready to pay for it. She looked up, surprised, mouth open to speak, before she closed it, a softening coming to her face. She was loved and cherished, she knew, and the angel would be a reminder of that, Brownie stated.

Brownie tucked their purchases into his truck and reached for Keegan's hand, walking them towards a small park. He had purchased sandwiches, fruit, and beverages for them, intending on a late autumn picnic. The day was warm and he was glad of that.

Keegan gathered the remains of their lunch and crumpled the papers together, feeling relaxing for the first time in a while, she thought. Brownie rose to dump the garbage and then pulled her to her feet. He walked them back towards the entrance to the park, breathing deeply of the fresh air. Little did he realize how things were about to change!

A noise drew his attention and he looked around and then up. Brownie frowned as he searched for the whining sound and what caused it. A drone, he thought, circling them. He shouted and then shoved at Keegan.

"Run, Keegan. Run for the truck. Call for help."

Brownie hesitated for just a moment, to watch to make sure that she was doing just that. Then, his feet pounded against the ground as he headed away from her. A sudden loud explosion sounded from behind him as a package hit the ground. Brownie's body flew forward to slam into the ground. He lay still, arms and legs askew, as the smoke cleared from around him.

Keegan had turned for a moment, intending to head back for him when the explosion happened. She flew backwards as well, to lay awkwardly on the ground. Her eyes fluttered as she tried to regain her consciousness, a battle that she tried hard to win. Her ears rung with the sound of the explosion.

Bystanders and park occupants spun at the sound of the explosion and then the men were racing towards the couples. On their knees they began to feel for signs of live. Children screamed and then hid against their mothers, afraid to look but afraid not to. Sirens could be heard and flashing lights seen as the emergency services rushed to the scene. Squealing brakes were heard as was scattering gravel as the sirens cut out, but the lights remained on.

One of the officers ran for Keegan, on his knees beside her, shock on her face.

"It's Keegan, Bob!" Her voice rang through the sudden hush and silence.

"Keegan? Where's Brownie?" Another officer stood for a moment staring at the crater from the explosion and then raised his eyes. "Brownie!"

Heads shot around and then there were calls for the paramedics. Some officers stayed with Keegan, some headed for the crater, and others headed for Brownie. Justin had been in the area and was one of the first to reach Brownie. He was on his knees and reached to feel for a pulse. Brownie was alive. How badly hurt he was? That was unknown at the present time.

With the paramedics now beside her, Justin was on his feet. He eyed Brownie for a moment before he headed to where Keegan was being assessed. He could see that she was trying hard to speak and knelt beside her.

"Keegan?" He waited, watching as she frantically twisted and turned, trying to escape the hands that were reaching to help her.

"Justin? Brownie? Oh, he's dead, isn't he? I just know that he is." Sobs almost choked her words off.

"No, he's not, Keegan. He is hurt, but he's not dead. What happened?" Justin waited almost impatiently, not sure if Keegan had heard him at all.

"A drone, I think Brownie said. He told me to run for the truck and he headed the other way. Only I didn't make it. I turned to try and find him just as whatever it was exploded." Tears flowed down her face as she sobbed. "I just know Brownie's dead. Why do they hate me so much?"

Justin frowned even as he looked at the female officer standing near him.

"Did she just say that, Justin?"

"She did, Lace. She did. I wonder who she meant?" Justin was on his feet, rubbing at his face before he pointed to Lace. "You ride with her. Stay with her wherever she goes."

Lace nodded. That had been her intent. Brownie had been a good friend of hers over the years. They had been classmates since early primary days.

"His family?" Justin looked around. "Bob, head for his parents. Bring them to the hospital. Have someone find Cami as well."

"We will." The officer moved away, stopping for a moment to turn and watch the frantic activity that was going on. Brownie was down and no one knew just how badly hurt he was. Keegan was injured but talking but that didn't mean that she wasn't seriously injured. They needed to find the ones responsible. Only that didn't seem to be happening.

$$\mathcal{Chapter\ 30}$$

The physician stood for a moment, his eyes on Keegan's chart, before he brushed back the curtain and approached her bed. She had quietened to some degree but was still restless. Imaging had been good, he thought. No broken bones. Soft tissue injuries, he thought. She seemed disoriented but that was to be expected given the explosion. The physician wanted to speak with her next of kin. Only that was Brownie. He frowned again as he heard footsteps stop beside him.

Justin looked between the physician, Dr. Jack Black, and Keegan. He knew the dilemma that Jack was facing.

"Jack? How is she?" Jack was Justin's cousin. "How is Keegan?"

"Remarkably lucky, I would say, Justin. God was there." Jack reached to assess her. "Soft tissue injuries. She is disoriented but that comes from being near the explosion."

"I see. Listen, she has no next of kin other than Brownie and his family. His mother is asking if she can come back with her."

"That should be fine." Jack looked at Keegan's records. "We can add Cameron and Cara to her records as next of kin. I know Brownie would be fine with that."

"Thanks, cuz. Now, Brownie?"

"Brownie. That's another case. Come on. I was heading there next." Justin moved to a nearby cubicle. "In here."

Justin watched Brownie for a moment, studying him, seeing that he was still out of it, as he termed it.

"How is he?"

Jack shook his head.

"I really can't tell yet. Let me see what the imaging shows and then we'll talk. I'll need to speak with his parents as well."

Jack studied the imaging, a frown in place. This was not what he wanted to see. Brownie would need surgery, with his internal bleeding. His right shoulder seemed to have taken the brunt of the fall and would require repair to it. A lot of bruising and soft tissue injuries would be the least of what he faced. Brownie would not be at work for a long while. How that would affect what Jack knew he was going through? That, he had no idea how Brownie would cope with that. With Keegan injured as well? That just threw more stress into the situation.

Justin stepped away, walking through the waiting room. He saw the men and women from the force moving around as they waited for word on their colleague and his bride. Cameron and Cara were seated near the entrance to the rooms, Cami standing leaning against the wall. He hesitated for a moment and then headed outside. Aaron was walking towards him, a takeout cup of coffee extended towards him.

"Thanks, Aaron." Justin sipped at it, his eyes on the sky. It was darkening into twilight.

"What happened? I just heard that they were hurt. I was out of town questioning a witness in another case."

"A bomb. Dropped by a drone. Brownie took the brunt of it. He's heading to surgery in a bit. Keegan is not as badly injured but she is not leaving here tonight." He sipped at his coffee, thoughts muddled for a moment.

"How do we keep them safe then, Justin? They are following them too closely, I suspect. What do you suggest?"

"Hide them away somewhere but where would that be? I know Brownie. He won't go. And Keegan is chafing at the bit to find the men responsible." Justin grimaced at the thought of what could happen. "How's the investigation coming?"

"It's coming but slow. We just have so many on the go right now. That I don't understand. We have never had this many at a time." Aaron was puzzled but he had a thought that he needed to mull over and do some research on.

"I would think that this is deliberate. You have so many but not enough information to solve them. That sounds deliberate to me." Justin waited for Aaron to respond, finally turning his head to watch him.

"I think you are correct, Justin. But how do we solve them? They all seem to be stalling."

"Talk to Emma. She's a consultant with our service. Or Evan. He knows the area now. Shay is another one to talk generalities with. Someone is setting us up and I would like to know why."

"I know they are." Aaron turned back to the hospital, eyeing the building. "We have many volunteers to stand guard over the next few days. Keegan's heading for a room?"

"I would suspect so. This is sad, you know." Justin's feet reluctantly took him towards the door. "She has no family other than Brownie's family. Did we ever track down her parents?"

"We did. They're not saying much, but someone is watching them. We saw evidence of that. And we don't know why."

"What's their connection to Walker or Baker?" Justin sighed as his phone chimed. He stared at the email. "Kat has come through. Walker is related to her mother, a cousin twice removed."

"That's interesting. Now maybe we can get somewhere. Has she sent you the information?"

"She has. To you as well as Brownie. Only, he won't be seeing it for a while." Justin was frustrated.

"No, he won't. But we can talk with Keegan over the next day or so."

"I wonder how many of those cases are related to Walker or Baker or even Edwin." Justin walked through the door, finding Cameron looking for him. "Cameron? What news?"

"Brownie has been taken to surgery. It will be a while. Keegan was not able to get in to see him.

She's sleeping right now but Jack said she'd be heading for a room soon." Cameron looked around. "There are so many of his colleagues here, Justin."

"They are. They want to help in some way. We have had to assign shifts for them to stand at the doors of the rooms. They will not leave them alone."

"I see. Listen, can we talk? Keegan was muttering something when we were in there. Something about her mother and a man named Walker."

"She was? What did she say?" Justin exchanged a glance with Aaron, who was listening intently.

"That she thought she had finally recognized Walker. That somehow she knew him from when she was young. That he had been around her mother. I am not sure how accurate her memory is, but I thought that you should know." Cameron walked away at that, heading for where Cami was waiting for him.

"That's interesting, Aaron, that she would remember that. Hidden memories coming to the surface." Justin just shook his head.

"They will come up and now that she has started to remember, they will come quicker and thicker." Aaron hesitated for a moment. "We need to figure out how to get her to remember without it destroying her."

Chapter 31

Walker hovered in the waiting room near the surgical suite. He was frustrated, that much was obvious. He tried hard to hide it but wasn't quite successful. Who had dropped that bomb? That was his question. He hadn't and he hadn't ordered it done. Was someone else involved? His eyes turned to the door and he moved away, heading for another floor and another waiting room. Walker was not aware that his employer had arranged that, as a warning to him, a warning that he never understood.

Standing in the full waiting room on the medical floor, Walker searched the people gathered. He knew many were police officers but others were not. His eyes narrowed for a moment as he spied one woman waiting. It was the woman from the other night. He needed to speak with her but he doubted that he would get a chance. He spun on his heels and walked away, not seeing that he was being followed. Aaron walked carefully behind him, searching the area as well, not sure if Walker had anyone with him. He wanted to catch him but a sudden influx of people coming through the main doors of the hospital separated him from his quarry. When Aaron made it outside, Walker was nowhere in sight. His hands clenched in frustration before he blew out a breath. Aaron was frustrated, to say the least.

Turning, he headed back towards the entrance of the hospital, stepping to one side to allow a woman to pass him. He felt a slight tug at his jacket pocket and another frown covered his face. He looked around and sighed. No, another one has disappeared on him.

Aaron headed for the coffee shop, knowing that he needed to eat but not willing to take the time to obtain a full meal in the cafeteria. He grabbed the sandwich that he wanted, a cup of coffee, and reached for his wallet. He pulled out the envelope, staring at it, before he spun to stare at the outside door. Shaking his head, Aaron gathered his food and headed for the floor that Brownie was on. He was worried about his friend, not having heard the latest.

Cameron stood at his son's bedside early in the morning. Brownie had come through his surgery and the repairs that needed to be made had been done. The internal bleeding had been stopped but the physicians were still concerned about him. Cameron's hand landed gently on his son's head as he prayed for healing for him and healing for Keegan. Cara was with Keegan, simply stating that she needed a mother and hers wasn't around.

Turning his head as he heard a slight noise, Cameron beckoned to Aaron.

"Aaron? You look troubled, son."

"I am, Cameron. How is Brownie?" Aaron stopped at the foot of the bed, his eyes on his friend and colleague.

"He's through his surgery. Now to heal. The surgeon said it would be a while though. They're concerned about a concussion and how that will affect him."

"That is a concern. He hasn't been awake at all?"

Cameron shook his head.

"Not yet. They don't expect it to be a while. Cara is with Keegan. That's why she's not here. But that's not why you're here." He turned his eyes to Aaron and then frowned. "Aaron, did you know that you had a paper sticking out of your pocket?"

Aaron stared at him and then down at his jacket. Cameron was right. It wasn't the envelope that he had already taken out but not yet opened. He set aside his cup of coffee and pulled out the paper. This was not what the woman had done then, he thought. Someone else had done this. He hadn't noticed it and that was not good. Not good at all. He opened it and read it, his face tightening for a moment as he did so.

"Aaron?"

"It's okay, Cameron. Just some new information that I need to track down. What can we do for you?" Aaron watched Cameron closely, seeing the fatigue in his face and in how he was standing.

Cameron shrugged, his eyes on the window where he could see the sun rising, brightening the day.

"Right now? I am not sure, Aaron. It's you and your fellow officers that need to be taken care of. This affects you all. All we can do right now is pray for you and for ourselves."

Aaron stayed for a little while longer before he was off. His head dropped for a moment as he drew in a deep breath. He had too many cases to work tight now, but he really needed sleep. He had been working on two or three hours a night for the last two weeks. Aaron looked up as he felt a hand on his shoulder. The lead detective, Matthias, stood there.

"Aaron? Head home and don't come in for twenty-four hours. You're off duty for now." Matthias watched as it took a few moments for Aaron to nod and then head for his vehicle. He watched closely and then turned to study the hospital. Shaking his head, he headed back for the detachment, knowing that he had work he needed to do.

Cameron walked away from Brownie, his head down as he struggled with his emotions. Never had he ever thought that Brownie would be so hurt. Sure, he acknowledged to himself, there was always a possibility of that happening but Brownie had always shrugged off his concern. He looked up to see Cara waiting for him and just reached to hug her.

"Cara?"

"How's Conor?"

"Still out of it. They think that he will be for a while. How Keegan?" He directed her to the waiting room and then sat, his arm around her.

"She's rousing. The physician, Amos, thought that she should be awake later today. How do we tell her about Conor?"

"God will give up the words, love. He always does. Now, I have to head off. Are you staying?"

"I am, for now. Cami said that she'd be around later but she had to head into work. Something about a project that needed her."

———

"She does have a deadline that she's working on." Cameron just sat, his eyes closing as he slumped backwards.

"Cameron?" Cara turned when he didn't answer and then just smiled. He was asleep and she would not awaken him. Her own eyes closed as she sat in prayer, prayer for her son and prayer for his wife, a lady who she had come to love deeply.

Neither one saw the couple around their own age that had entered the area and then sat, staring around. The couple spoke quietly for a few moments before the man rose and headed away. He wanted information on Keegan, only he had no idea who to ask.

Chapter 32

A day later, Keegan was on her feet, shaking her head as the nurses tried to keep her in her bed. She dressed, walked away, and headed for Brownie. Cara linked an arm with hers, helping keep her upright.

"Are you sure that you should be up?" Cara's question was quietly spoken, but Keegan knew that Cara supported her decision.

"I have to, Cara. I have to. Brownie needs me." Keegan walked slowly towards the elevator, intent on finding Brownie. "I have to find him. I need to."

Cara nodded, knowing that if it had been her, she would have been determined to reach Cameron. She walked with the younger woman, stopping in the doorway as Keegan moved forward. She could hear conversation behind her and turned as she felt a presence there that had just stopped. Cara frowned at the man who stood there, thinking that he reminded her of someone. Just who that was, she wasn't sure.

Keegan approached the bed, a hand to her mouth as she stared at her husband. This was not what she had expected, to see the bruising and the bandages. Nor did she expect all the monitors or the nasal prongs that provided him the oxygen that was needed.

———

165

A hand rested on his cheek before she bent to kiss his forehead. *Lord, please? Heal him? And quickly? I need him so much.* Keegan's eyes raised to search the room, feeling evil somewhere near her. Her eyes sought out the equipment, hearing the soft beeps, not understanding what the readings were.

The nurse approached the bed, moving around it, her eyes resting on Keegan every once in a while. She left and then returned with a wheelchair. Touching Keegan's shoulder, she pointed to the chair.

"Here, Keegan. I've brought in a wheelchair for you to use. Please, sit. You don't have to leave right now but at some point, we will send you back to your room. You need to rest as well in order to heal from your injuries."

Keegan hesitated and then sank gratefully into it. The nurse was right. She couldn't stand that long.

Cara appeared, a hand resting on Keegan's head. Aaron had been heading her way, she has seen, and wanted to warn her.

"How is Conor?"

Keegan shrugged, not sure what to say.

"The nurse said he was coming along as well as they could expect." She swiped at the tears on her cheeks. She hated to cry but seemed to be doing that a lot later. She felt defeated and beaten down.

"It will take a while, love. He was hurt badly. But he would be thankful that he took the force of the blast and you didn't."

"I know. But it's not fair. Brownie shouldn't have done that." She looked around, not sure what to say next. "Has Aaron been around?"

"He has been. In fact, he's out in the waiting room right now, wanting to speak with you."

Keegan sighed. Lord, I can't do this. Is this the path that You have for us to walk? I can't do this. Not any more. I just can't. Brownie has been hurt because of me. I need to have him heal. Do I need to leave him for him to be safe?

Aaron stood for a moment watching Keegan before he pulled up a chair and sat, his portfolio landing on the table beside him. He watched Brownie for a moment, trying to assess how he was. He shook his head, knowing that it would be a while before Brownie awakened. As to what he did after that? It was up in the air. It would depend on how Brownie healed in all ways.

Keegan turned her head, waiting for the vertigo to stop before she spoke.

"Aaron?"

"Keegan? How are you?" Aaron gave a smile. "About like that?"

Keegan thought about nodding and decided against it.

"Yeah, about like that. I don't like this vertigo." She sighed. "What have you to say? Where do we stand with the investigation?"

Aaron nodded. Her words were what he had expected her to say.

"Not where we want to be. Listen, we have tracked down your parents."

"You have? I had no idea where they were or even if they were still alive. We parted ways years ago." Keegan blinked for a moment. "I haven't seen them for years. Where were they?"

"In a town near you. I haven't had a chance to speak with them, but I was told that they were heading this way. They apparently have some information for us. You would not be aware that your mother is related to Walker."

"She is? No, I wouldn't have known that. They never talked about their family. I know their parents were dead. Now what?"

"Now what? We meet with your parents and get their side of the story. Then we talk with you about it. You need to stay alert. Walker has been around here, waiting for a chance to nab you."

Keegan nodded, her eyes sliding closed as she slumped for a moment, fatigue and pain getting the better of her.

"Where do I go, Aaron? I won't leave Brownie. Not at all." Her eyes slid over to Brownie and she was on her feet, her hand on his cheek as he moved restlessly. "What about Brownie? How safe is he? They'll go after him to get to me, won't they?"

"They will. We have officers outside his door and they will be with you. We're coming to the crunch time, Keegan." Aaron watched her closely. "We'll do our best to keep you safe."

———

"I know you will, but will your best be good enough?"

Chapter 33

Three days later, Brownie's head moved restlessly on the pillow as he began to rouse. Keegan watched him, a hand on his, the other hand on his cheek. She wanted him to be awake and not to be hurt, just like a few days ago. Only, that would not happen. She prayed for peace for what they were going through and for healing for Brownie. Keegan really didn't care about herself.

Keegan was puzzled, to tell the truth. She had no idea that her mother was related to Walker and had been shocked when Aaron told her that. She wanted to talk it over with Brownie, to hear him tell her that it wasn't her fault. But right at the moment? Only, Brownie couldn't do just that.

Brownie's eyes opened slowly and then closed again after the light. It hurt, he thought. He felt a hand on his face and turned towards it.

"Brownie? Are you waking up? Please, Brownie. I need you to. Lord, please? Let him awake. I need him to." Keegan's voice was thick with tears and she raised a hand to swipe them away.

"Keegan? Where am I?" Brownie finally focused on his bride's face.

"You're in the hospital, Brownie. You were hurt a few days ago. Don't you remember?"

Brownie blinked, trying to remember.

"No, I'm sorry, I don't. Were you hurt?" Brownie reached to touch her face, finding a stray tear that he flicked away.

"Not really. I am so worried about you."

Brownie gave a deep sigh. He didn't quite understand what she meant but he struggled to focus on her face. He frowned, bringing on his headache once more. As he tried to move, he felt the pain in his shoulder.

"What happened, sweetheart?" His eyes slid closed as he tried to control the pain.

"Someone dropped a bomb from a drone. You sent me one way and ran the other. You didn't make it in time and were hurt."

"Were you?" Brownie reached to raise the head of the bed, his eyes sliding closed for a moment before he simply wrapped his good arm around her, not caring about the IV lines attached to it.

"Not really." She hugged him back, keeping in mind his shoulder. "I was so worried, Brownie. You aren't going to be working for a while. What did I do?"

"You did nothing, sweetheart. Once I'm out of here, we'll track down whoever it is and bring them to justice."

"I know. I just wish…" She let her voice fall away. "Brownie? What are we do?" Keegan was repeating herself.

Brownie looked past her, a frown on his face. Walker stood in the doorway, a smirk on his face as he watched them. He disappeared from view before

———

Brownie could say anything. Next thing he knew, Aaron was walking into the room.

"Walker was just here, Aaron." Brownie pointed at the door, not letting go of Keegan.

Aaron was gone, hunting for Walker and not finding him. He was frustrated by not finding him. He walked back towards the room before he detoured, looking for a security guard and then following him to the security area.

Brownie moved his hand to drop the bed rail, watching with slight amusement as Keegan just crawled up beside him. His arm tightened around her as she leaned back, an elbow planted on the bed and her head on her hand. He reached to raise the bed rail once more before his arm tightened again around his bride. Brownie watched her face before he reached to kiss her.

Keegan was puzzled. She didn't understand what was happening, hat she knew. How was her mother involved? And was her father involved as well? She never really understood what had happened all those years ago. And she had no way to contact her mother or her father. Any contact information was lost

Aaron moved towards them, a frown on his face. He had found the video of Walker but could not find him anywhere in the hospital. Frustration was uppermost in his mind. Aaron needed to talk with Keegan but he wasn't sure just how to go about it or even what she would remember. He stood for a moment, watching Keegan and then Brownie, finding Brownie watching him in turn.

———

"Brownie? You're awake?"

"I am. For now." Brownie studied Aaron and then Keegan. He sighed. His eyes drifted closed and he slept, not seeing Keegan moving away from him.

Keegan dropped back to her feet, a hand on Brownie's shoulder before she looked at Aaron. *Lord, now what? What is this path that I'm supposed to be walking that I don't want to? I know that You are here and in control. I am trying too hard to trust, dear Lord, but I have so much trouble doing that. Please, Lord? Lead me. Lead Brownie. And lead Aaron and his team to the answers.*

"Keegan? We need to talk." Aaron pointed to a chair. "Sit. It's going to take some time."

"I know, Aaron. I know." Keegan blinked, her eyes on the window, watching the dark clouds that were gathering and the high wind that was moving the trees in a wild manner. A storm was brewing outside, she thought, and in here a well.

"Keegan?" Aaron waited patiently, his notebook out. "What can you tell me about your family? As in aunts, uncles, cousins, grandparents."

Keegan shrugged, her mind not on what he was asking.

"I don't know. I am not sure that I know who they are. Mom and Dad didn't talk much about their family. I never knew their parents. Nor any of their siblings. I'm sorry." Keegan blinked rapidly, trying to clear her vision of the tears that clouded it. She stared at the machines around Brownie and then at the nurse who had entered and moved quietly around, doing her assessment of Brownie. "He's been awake, nurse."

"Thank you, Keegan. That is good to know. Now, how are you? What can I get for you?" She smiled as Keegan blinked at her in surprise.

"I don't know. Maybe a resolution to what we're going through. Can you do that?"

The nurse gave a gentle smile.

"We would do that, Keegan, if we could. All of us are trying to help. Brownie is well known here in town for helping, for giving of himself to anyone who needs his help. That's the character of your husband."

Chapter 34

Brownie moved slowly around his home a few days later. He was hurting but had decided against the prescription medication. It was late evening or early morning, he corrected himself, squinting at the clock on the mantle of the fireplace. He headed for bed, not sure that he would even sleep. He stood for a moment, his eyes on Keegan before they lifted and he stared at the framed photo of a local rundown mill that he had on the wall above the bed. Determination coloured his face before he too sought his rest, his arm out to wrap around Keegan and draw her close to him. Brownie's head rested against hers as he prayed for them both and for those working their adventure.

Keegan arose the next morning, pausing for a moment to rest a hand on Brownie's cheek. A sad smile covered her face before she too stared at the wall. Determination flowed through her. Today? Today, she would find out what she could on her family. Evan had been around, suggesting a friend of his, a lady named Kat, who might be able to help. Keegan rested her mug on the porch railing as she stared out across the yard, not seeing the early morning activity but hearing it. She sighed. *This is definitely not how she planned her life, now was it, Lord? But I know that You have walked the path before me and know exactly what we face. Help me to trust, dear Lord. This is difficult for me. You know that I do have trust issues that are long standing, and trust is what I need to do. Help me to trust in You with all my heart. You know the longings and dreams that I have even better than you. Please, Lord?*

Reaching for her phone, Keegan sighed. There were a number of text messages, voice mails, and email messages. She felt overwhelmed for a moment, her eyes closing as she struggled to control her emotions, not sure if she even could.

Brownie had arisen, struggled to dress and then sought for his bride. He stood, watching the emotions flickering across her face and sighed. How did they do this? He was handicapped for now with the injury to his shoulder and that fact frustrated him beyond anything that he had ever experienced. He walked forward on almost silent socked feet to just wrap her in his arms, his chin resting on the top of her head. He prayed audibly for just her, trusting that God heard the unspoken words in his heart.

"Keegan, sweetheart? What's wrong?" Brownie spoke at long last.

"I don't know, Brownie. I just wish that I could run away and not be found anywhere. It's gotten so dangerous." Keegan held up her phone. "There are just so many messages. I don't know where to start."

Brownie reached and gently removed the phone from her hand, placing it on a colourful, leaf-patterned placement on his light oak table and hugged her tighter. Keegan struggled to turn in his arms, wrapping hers around him. He could feel the tears soaking into his shirt but didn't care. The love of his life just needed to be held and that he could do, even with only one arm.

Brownie eventually reached to shove her into a chair and then for her phone. He moved quietly away to retrieve a pad of paper and pen before he sat beside her. His eyes on her, he reached for the phone.

"We'll go through each one, starting with the text messages. It might not be as bad as you think."

Keegan shrugged, reaching for the pen.

"Let's get started. Then, maybe we can figure it out."

They listened to the voice mail, a frown on Brownie's face once in a while. He nodded as he heard Aaron asking to meet with them today. Keegan made a note to call him in a bit, if he didn't show up.

Brownie sat back as they finished. Most of the messages were from friends or his colleagues. But one had caused Keegan distress. It was from a family friend who she had kept somewhat in contact with. Kevin had simply asked if he could speak with Keegan, that the police had been around and questioned them, and he felt that he had to talk with her. Would she call him?

Keegan stared at the number and then at Brownie.

"I don't know what he would want. I never had much contact with him, but I know he had my number."

Brownie nodded, knowing that he would ask Aaron to contact the man, not letting Keegan. He looked up as the doorbell rang and Keegan was on her feet. He rose, making a fresh pot of coffee, hearing Keegan's surprised voice. He turned as he heard Keegan returning, seeing Tag and Ayron with her.

"Tag? You're here?"

"We are. We're here to help. Evan's and Shay's are heading this way. I also heard from Micah. He and Kat are heading here as well." Tag looked at Keegan, a grin crossing his face, as he saw Ayron moving towards the counter, setting down the bags that she had been carrying. "Kat has a family tree program that she has been working on for you. They'll be here in about an hour or so. We've talked about them and what they do."

Keegan stared at Tag and then Ayron before she threw up hands.

"Sure, why not? This house has been a busy highway, hasn't it?" She glared at the three as they laughed at her. "Well, it is."

Brownie's arm wrapped around her even as he tried to control his laughter.

"It's okay, sweetheart. It's a big house and we'll manage. For now, let's sit down with Tag and Ayron and see what we can accomplish." He looked around as he heard the door open and Aaron appeared, dressed casually in jeans and a sweatshirt. "Aaron? Aren't you working?"

Aaron grinned at the disgruntled look on Keegan's face.

"I am. I have been told to work only on your case and to stay away from the office. So, can we set up an office here?"

Brownie grinned.

"We can." He pointed to the coffee pot. "That's fresh. Ayron, what do you have?"

"Food!" She grinned, knowing that she and Brownie had done this many times, sharing a meal together. "We need to keep up our strength." She frowned at him, her brows drawing down. "And you need your pain medications."

"I know, Ayron. I know. It's just that they make me sleepy, and I need to be alert."

Keegan turned to him, a frown on her own face.

"Yes, you're taking them. And we'll work with you as we can. But if you need to sleep, Brownie, you need to sleep."

Late that afternoon, Keegan walked back after closing the door behind their younger guests. Cameron and Cara were around, she knew, Cameron with Brownie in his home office. Cara had gone out to the yard, not wanting to intrude on the kitchen. Keegan sighed to herself. This is awkward, she thought, as she walked through the hallway, her feet almost silent on the dark oak flooring. She hesitated before she took walked outside, finding Cara waiting for her, an arm out to hug her.

"Keegan? What can we do for you?"

Keegan shrugged, tears in her eyes. A mom, she thought, who wants to help me. When did I last feel that?

Chapter 35

A week later, Aaron stood back from his house door, watching Tag and Evan approach him. This can't be good, he thought. He had spent the morning with Brownie, getting no further ahead in his investigation. He was going to have to drop it, unless something happened. Brownie had commented that they weren't getting what usually happened, the parcels, the threats, the letters, the pictures. In fact, he had not seen Walker around.

"Aaron? We need to talk." Evan's face was grim.

"About what?" He pointed back towards his office. "Brownie?"

"Brownie? I found some information that is disturbing, about Keegan. About her parents."

"Her parents?" Aaron sank into his chair, his hand out for the papers Tag was shoving at him.

"Her parents. Has she said much? I don't know much about them."

"Not really. She said that they just disappeared one day and she couldn't find them. I have spoken with a family friend." Aaron couldn't say what they had talked about but Aaron was concerned deeply about that couple. It appeared that they may not have disappeared on their own.

"Yeah, her parents." Tag sat back, a frown covering his face for a moment. "I spoke with Emma. She's found them, she tells me."

"She has?" Aaron sat forward. "And who is Emma?"

"Emma Finlay. I work for her." Evan sighed, knowing what he had to say. "I imagine that you are familiar with Tracker's? That's Emma. She finds people no one else can and can't explain how she does it."

"I have heard of her. I didn't know that you worked for her." Aaron studied the papers. He was impressed with what he read. "How does she does this?"

"She can't explain it. Her husband, Abe, runs a security team and has offered security for Brownie and Keegan if they need to. You've met Micah and Kat. Micah works for Abe. And yes, they all had what they considered adventures."

"They have?" Aaron's gaze stopped on an address. "This address? This is where they are? Have they been there long?"

Tag shook his head.

"No, they were moved there just as Keegan and Brownie met. They had been kept way back in the boonies as we say, no contact with many people. They were essentially slaves for this person." He reached over to tap the paper laying on the top of the pile. "This proves it. Aaron said the authorities in that area were moving in. We just don't have the information that we need to confirm why they were taken or how it relates to Keegan."

———

"It has to relate in some way." Aaron stood and paced, thinking better on his feet and moving. He stopped to grab the papers and read through them as he walked, his steps slowing as he neared the last one. The names on it clicked and he knew then why Keegan and Brownie had been targeted. He just had to prove it and prove it he would. And it would be soon. That much he was determined to do.

"Aaron? Where do we go?" Evan rose and approached him.

"For now, I need to talk to her parents, but I can't right now. They're with another force and that's being investigated. I'll reach out to the force." Aaron turned to look at Evan and then past him at Tag.

"We can do that. Emma's telling me to work on this full time for now and she's doing the same." Evan was frustrated as well.

"That we will do." Tag spun in a circle and headed for the door, running for his car. He had a thought and rifled through what paperwork he had in his briefcase. A satisfied sound came from him and he turned and ran for the house. "Listen, guys. I have this. I don't know where it came from, but I think it's related to what we've been looking into."

The two other men spun and stared at him.

"What is it?" Aaron reached for the papers, hope in his heart.

"A name and details about him. Ayron was working away last night, searching for what she couldn't tell me. She found Keegan's graduation yearbook on the internet. The one from her college and one from her high school. She had been praying about who it was and these three people stood out to her. I began my investigation and I don't like what I found."

Aaron's hand froze for a moment in its forward motion before he took the papers. Is this it, Lord? Will this solve it? He sighed as his phone chimed. It had been doing that on and off all day. He looked at the text. Keegan and then Brownie.

"Guess what, guys? They just got a package. Keegan opened it before Brownie could stop her. She's devastated, Brownie says, and Keegan says that she's angry."

"What was in it?" Evan and Tag shared a look as Evan spoke

"And are they alone?" Tag turned, almost ready to head for that home.

"No. Shay and Breckon are there." Aaron ran his hands through his hair after dropping his phone to his desk. "Let's work through this and then I'll head there."

"No, we take this and go there. What they received is important. Did they say what was in it?" Evan was beginning to gather the papers, looking around for something to stuff them into it. He took the envelope that Aaron handed him with thanks. "Let's head there"

"Wait a moment, Evan." Tag stared at the floor, his fingers rubbing together. "This is important but what was it exactly that was in the package?"

"Neither said, but Brownie said it was enough
to almost shut Keegan down." Aaron locked his door
and headed for his car. "Let's go."

———

Chapter 36

Keegan shook violently as she stood at their kitchen table, her eyes focused on the package that she had opened. It had been addressed to her and had a return address from a friend who knew that she was married. Only, the contents were not what she would have expected from her friend. Brownie's good arm was around her as he studied her and then the box.

Shay shared a look with Breckon before he spoke.

"Do you know this Karen?" His eyes rested on Keegan, a frown on his face as he studied her and then turned to Brownie.

"I know her. She's a friend. But she wouldn't do this." Keegan pointed at the box. "She just wouldn't." She blinked rapidly, a frown covering her face. "These photos? They came from my home. She has no access to it."

Brownie sighed. This was something that they had talked about but had had no chance to follow through.

"Your home? We've already cleared it out. You have nothing left there. Your parents' home? It's rented, you said."

Keegan nodded, her hair brushing against Brownie's face. She lifted her eyes to Breckon, seeing the compassion and caring on her new friend's face.

"Why? Who would do this?"

"Walker. He's upping his game, knowing that he hasn't been able to get to you. You've been too well protected." Shay nodded at Brownie. "And no, we're not putting you out there. Not yet. Aaron, Evan, and Tag are on their way over here."

"And Flannery and Ayron are on the way as well. We'll figure it out." Breckon turned to the kitchen. "I'm on food duty. Keegan, what can we use? Do we need to do a food run?"

"No, I think we're good. I have a huge crock pot of chili on and there are lots of dessert stuff. There is also stuff for salads. The only thing we would need is fresh bread."

"Fresh bread? Do you have a bread maker?" Breckon paused in the kitchen, looking around.

"In the pantry." Keegan pointed to the door. "Just look through the cupboards and find what you need." She abruptly headed for the back door and disappeared through it. She was feeling totally overwhelmed and her emotions were all over the place.

Breckon watched her, a sad smile on her face. She could understand to a certain extent how she felt. She turned as she heard many footsteps and watched all the men appear, with Flannery and Ayron in the forefront.

"Keegan?" Brownie looked for her, sadness on his face as he thought through what had just happened.

"Outside." Breckon reached out a hand to stop him. "Let us ladies talk to her. I have bread in the bread maker for our meal but I'll take the time to speak with her. So will Flannery and Ayron."

"Thanks, ladies. If it will help, go for it."

Ayron and Flannery headed for the back door, stopping to grab a tray with coffees on it. Breckon headed after them in a few minutes, stopping to speak quietly with Aaron.

Aaron looked around before he headed for the office, dropping his files on the desk and then sitting behind it. He looked around as Brownie entered and dropped into a chair in front of the desk.

"Brownie, what all was in the box? I gather that you took pictures before the techs took it?"

"I did. I've uploaded them to a file on the desktop. However, it has really distressed Keegan. I can't have that." His eyes slid closed as he fought his emotions. "There were pictures of her over her life since she was 18. A threat that her life was forfeited now that she was married." He looked at Aaron, devastation on her face. "Who does this? And why now with the photos?"

"I have no idea, Brownie, but I suspect we're getting close to who they are. I spoke with the detective in her hometown. She has her parents tucked away safely and is in the process of debriefing them. It will take time. They are so worried about Keegan."

———

"They are? She was so certain that they didn't want her. That had always puzzled her. There hadn't seemed to be problems before that. Why did they wait until she was 18?"

"Until she was of legal age. That's why. But the question is what did they want?" Aaron looked around as he heard a sound and saw Shay entering the room.

"Shay?"

"That sounds like what happened with Ayron and Tag. Someone wanted Ayron to marry his son or even himself and they waited until her father was dead until they upped their game plan."

Brownie was nodding.

"That's right. He was brutal with what he planned." He paused, a thoughtful look on his face. "Aaron, what information and proof do you have?"

"Not what we need. We know that Walker is involved but we haven't got to the main person yet."

"It's going to be a relative, Brownie." Tag handed over papers. "This is her family tree as we have it. There are some suspects on that and Emma and Jace are working on those, just because we're close friends."

"That's good. Now, where do we go from here? How is Walker related to Keegan?" Shay felt like he was running to catch up on the details.

"He's a second cousin, a cousin twice removed, something like that." Aaron looked around for a moment. "Does he have family that we don't know about?"

Chapter 37

Aaron stood for a moment before the door of a house in Keegan's hometown. He looked around, feeling himself watched. He knew Walker had followed him as he had seen his car in his rearview mirror. That was okay with him, as long as it kept Brownie and Keegan safe.

He turned as the door opened and a woman who looked so much like Keegan stood there.

"Can I help you? You must have the wrong house." Her voice was low and sounded sad and defeated.

"No, I have the right place. You're Keegan's mother, Laura."

"I am." Laura seemed surprised. "But I don't know you."

A male voice sounded behind her.

"Who is it, dear?"

Aaron's identification was out as Keegan's father, Randy, appeared.

"I'm Aaron, the detective working Brownie and Keegan's case. Brownie is a really good friend of mine as well. May I come in?" Aaron waited.

"Sure. Come in. I'm sorry that this isn't our home but I understand that we can't go there right now. That it's not safe." Randy closed the door behind Aaron and pointed to the living room. "This is a temporary place for us, so we're not real comfortable here. The last ten years or more have not treated us kindly."

"No, I hear that they haven't." Aaron sat, assessing the couple that sat in front of him. He could see the weight of what they had been through in their faces and in how they moved. They had had a rough life the last few years and for what?

"What can we do for you?" Laura spoke quietly, almost too low to be heard, her hand reaching for Randy's.

"First, can we pray? We need that, I know."

Randy and Laura shared a look before their heads were bowed. Aaron prayed and then Randy followed. Aaron hesitated when they were done before he raised his head. This would be difficult for them to hear.

"Aaron?" Randy's voice broke into his thoughts. "Our daughter? You said you know my daughter?"

"I do. She is married to a really good friend of mine. His name is Conor but we call him Brownie. As to why, I am not sure. We've served on the police force together for years. He is a patrol officer."

"I see." Randy's hands rubbed together as he stared down at the worn carpet under his feet. "She was always adamant that she would never marry into law enforcement."

"He rescued her and then married her, knowing that he loved her but not sure if she did. She does, very much. However, they are not through whatever it is that they are involved in."

"The police detective here mentioned that. What exactly has been going on?" Laura's voice was still hesitant, as if she was not sure that she should be asking what was happening to their daughter. "I know that we had grown distant to some extent before we were locked away against our will. We thought we were just dealing with a teenager."

"You were and someone took advantage of that." Aaron opened his folder, hesitation not unlike him in his movements. "This goes very deep and back a ways, I think."

Beginning to speak, Aaron detailed what he could of the life that Brownie and Keegan had been living in the last few weeks. Randy and Laura both were shocked and looks of horror covered their faces.

"You mean, someone tried to kill them? With a bomb? And a drone?" Randy sat back, hands rubbing down his face.

"They did. Brownie was hurt the worst and is recovering. They are skirting around us, not saying much, neither one of them. I can understand that, but we need them to talk to us." Aaron looked around. "Have they told you how long that they need you to stay here?"

"I am not sure." Laura spoke, her hand brushing away the tears on her face. "They have said that they don't want us around Keegan for now, but I need to see my daughter. I need to apologize to her for not being there."

"It will come, Laura. But for now, you need to stay here where we can keep you safe."

Aaron stood at long last on the pavement beside his car. He looked around, not feeling the evil that he did when he was near Brownie and Keegan. That feeling was getting stronger and stronger each day and he feared for them. Randy and Laura had been a wealth of information regarding Walker, but Laura was puzzled as to why he was involved. She had not seen him for years and couldn't understand why he had taken Keegan hostage or captive or whatever word described it.

He reached for his phone and smiled. Keegan had sent a text message, just to say thanks and that he needed to get some rest. He had more cases than theirs to work on. *No,* he thought, *no, I don't, Keegan. This has been made my priority for now. It's coming to a close. Only, I fear that you may not survive or that Brownie may not survive.*

Sliding behind the wheel of his car, he drove away, watchful for anyone following him and not seeing anyone. He knew that Justin wanted to meet with him, to get a sense of when he felt Brownie would be returning to work. Only, he wasn't sure that Brownie would do that or even could do that. That man was jumping at the slightest noise as could be expected. Aaron knew that Keegan was trying her best to cope but was not doing so well herself. She was worried about herself but mores, was worried about Brownie, not knowing when the next attack would happen.

The sunlight blinded him for a moment and then clarity in the case hit. He knew who was behind it, thanks to his talk with Randy and Laura and the help Evan and Tag had provided. He just needed to prove it. That meant a trip to find Emma and Kat. Tomorrow, he thought, as he yawned. He had not been sleeping well, not worrying about his friend. This was coming to the climax or crisis or whatever it was that it could be called.

Chapter 38

Keegan was restless and her pacing in the house showed it. She had cleaned what she could. There was no baking that needed to be done. She had already baked more than she or Brownie needed and passed on the excess to friends and neighbours. Bored, Keegan moved towards the office, seeing Brownie hunched over the desk, a hand rubbing at his shoulder.

"Brownie? What can I do to help?" She stood with a hand on his uninjured shoulder. A small squeak escaped her as his arm came out and wrapped around her, drawing her down on Brownie's lap.

"Help me? I'm not sure what you mean." His eyes watched her closely, a frown on his face, masking the pain for a moment.

"Yes, help. What can I do to sort out that material that you seem so fascinated with? Is there some order that we need to put it in?" Keegan poked a finger at it.

Brownie grinned, his arm tightening around her.

"I don't know that it's in any order and it should be. I like how you think, sweetheart." He didn't move to release her and she settled back against his shoulder, one arm around his neck, careful of his injury.

"What about paper on the walls?" Keegan stared at the walls, knowing what she was asking. "Isn't that what they always do in books and movies if they're not the police and don't have white boards to work with?"

"We can do that, sweetheart." Brownie finally rose, heading for the closet in that room. Keegan was beside him, reaching for the paper and then looking around.

"Which room?"

"In here. That way we can leave the rest of the house somewhat normal." Brownie was frustrated in not being able to help as Keegan unrolled the paper. He reached for the tape, the roll in one hand as he ripped of pieces to tape the paper to the walls that Keegan had removed the framed pictures and diplomas from. He stared at his one diploma, showing when he graduated from college with his police degree. It saddened Brownie. He had been having nightmares about going back to work and just how he could do that. He was coming to the conclusion that he couldn't.

Keegan stopped in her movements before she stood beside Brownie, a hand on his back, a prayer raising for her beloved groom. She had a good idea of what his thoughts were.

"Brownie?" Her voice was quiet but still reached to him.

"Keegan? I need to make some decisions but I am not sure how to or even what."

"We'll pray it through, love. We'll pray it through." Keegan bit at her lip. "Have you heard from Aaron today?"

Brownie nodded, knowing what she wasn't asking.

"He is in court today and likely tomorrow as well. He said he'd try and drop by tonight, if he could. He has some information for us."

"Okay." Keegan moved away, reaching for the papers on the desk. "How do we do this? Sort by name? Date? Incident?"

"I think by date first and then by name and then incident."

They worked away quietly, with few comments between them, for most of the day. Brownie finally stepped back and stared at the walls. It was beginning to make sense. He turned as Keegan stopped beside him, a marker held in the air. He wrapped an arm around her, a kiss dropped on her temple.

"Does this make any sense?" Keegan felt defeated.

"It does. Let's take a break. We've been working on this all day and need that." He turned her around and headed for the kitchen. "We need to eat. Let's fix something and head outside."

Aaron watched Keegan closely an hour later, taking with thanks the plate of food Brownie handed him. He sat, his head bowed in prayer, before he began to eat. He watched as Keegan walked away, leaving Brownie staring after her, his heart on his face.

"Aaron? You have news?" Brownie slid a mug of coffee onto to table for Aaron and then sat himself.

"I do. I need to talk with Keegan. This is good. I didn't get a chance to grab any lunch." Aaron watched Brownie this time, seeing the stress lining his face. "Brownie? How are you really doing?"

"Wanting this over. I know it's not. I've seen evidence of someone around here, footsteps in the gardens, the back gate open when it was closed. In fact, there was a letter in the mail today. I haven't opened it yet. I was waiting for you." Brownie rose and retrieved the letter. "Keegan doesn't want to know what it contains."

"No, I don't, Aaron, but I know that I have to." Keegan stopped in the kitchen doorway, arms wrapped around her abdomen. She studied the soft yellow of the kitchen walls and the off-white cabinets. These were colours that she would have chosen.

"We'll talk, Keegan." Aaron paused, his fork in the air before he ate that forkful of food. "This is good."

"Thank you." Keegan walked away, not sure what to say.

"Aaron, what didn't you say?" Brownie's gaze shifted between Aaron and where he knew Keegan was waiting.

Sighing, Aaron studied his meal before he pushed away his plate.

"I spoke with her parents. I can let you both know some of what they said, but there is information that they provided that needs to be kept quiet."

Keegan faced the papers that they had taped to the walls, her fingers on her mouth. Somewhere here was the answer. Only she didn't know what. Brownie's arm was around her as he too studied the papers. Aaron approached the wall, his finger tracing names and then dates. He nodded. *They're solving it, aren't they, Lord? And what I can share will move it forward. His phone was out to take photos of their work.*

"Aaron, what can you add?" Keegan spoke softly, her eyes on him.

"Can we sit? This will take a while, I think." Aaron gathered his thoughts, his hand reaching for the folder with his notes. "I spoke with your parents, Keegan." He watched with compassion as her eyes slid closed.

"You did? And?" Her eyes popped open. "What excuse did they give?"

"I need you to listen to me for a few moments, Keegan. They did not willingly disappear. We did discuss that, I think." At her nod, he turned his attention to Brownie. "They were forced away from your home just as you turned 18. Your mom said that they were having what they thought were usual teenage years. It wasn't. Someone was feeding them false information. You didn't talk with them and that distressed them."

"I know. I just didn't know how to talk to them. They seemed so distant and I didn't know how to talk to them. It was a confusing time. I think that someone was also doing that to me, driving a wedge between us." Keegan blinked rapidly. "What did I do?"

"You did nothing. Someone did that to you. Now, I need to tell you what I can of their story. There is some information that I can't share with you. You know that. But first, Brownie?"

Brownie nodded, his head bowing as he prayed for peace and confidence in the path that they were walking, knowing that the Lord had already walked ahead of them.

Chapter 39

Keegan raised her head, her eyes on the wall, as she listened to Aaron rustling through his papers. She knew that he wanted to speak with her, but she was just so uncertain if she wanted to hear what he had to say. This was a turning point in her life, she acknowledged. She also knew that Walker had been hovering close to her. She had felt his presence when she was out and about in the town, thinking that at any point, he would just grab her and disappear with her. They would find her body somewhere, maybe, someday.

"Keegan? Your parents had a message for me to relay to you. They wanted to say that they were so sorry about what happened. It was out of their control. They were hidden away in the woods, not allowed to leave the small plot of land that they were on. Your father was forced to do the paperwork for the thefts of lumber and anything else. He is working with an investigator on that. He has been able to retain some documents that prove he was an unwilling participant in this. Your mother? She just existed, as she put it.

"Now, on to Walker. Your mom said that she had not seen him in years, avoiding him is how she phrased it. He had always been a troublemaker since he was a small child. She didn't want you around him. He is not directly related to you, an adopted child of her second cousin. She cannot think what he wants from you."

"To marry me. That's what I heard him say. He thought that if he married me and threatened me, that I would not say anything. He was so wrong. I want him brought to justice." Keegan raised her eyes to Aaron.

"We're working on it. Walker would come around where your parents were, letting them see him, and taunting them. They were afraid that he had already harmed you. They were not aware that you had escaped him many times. More times than you even know. We've been tracing his steps and he was so close to you. When he took you captive and Brownie as well, he saw a chance to destroy you and keep you captive. He had plans for you that you don't want to know about."

Keegan paled at that, her face burrowing against Brownie.

"I have a good idea of what that was. He was open in talking with Baker." She frowned. "How did Baker fit in?"

"Just another criminal and not a good one at that. Walker was not the head of the operation. He was just one of the men being used in theft. The theft of the valuable trees was just one part of what they were involved in."

Brownie stared down at Keegan, his thoughts racing.

"How deep into town are they?" He looked up as Aaron didn't speak. "That deep?"

Aaron nodded.

"That deep. We're gathering our information and verifying it. I think within the week that we can start making arrests. We need to keep you two out of sight and safe."

"That's not going to be possible, Aaron. We won't hide. It's taking too much from us to continue to do that. Keegan needs some freedom and I intend to give her that."

"I know. Colleagues have agreed to be there when you are out and about. They will be outside your home. This is the most dangerous portion of what we are facing with you."

"I know, Aaron. I've seen it too many times to not know that." Brownie rested his head on Keegan's, worried about the love of his life.

Aaron left at long last, not satisfied that he had made any progress. He thought back through the papers that had lined the office wall and grinned. Keegan was good. She had sorted it all through without really understanding what she had found. That had been evident from her comments. Brownie had simply shaken his head at him, knowing that Keegan had known what she was doing. She was trying her best to find the one responsible, without knowing the town. It tied back to her town as well, Aaron thought, and sighed. This just seemed to get bigger and bigger.

He dropped his paperwork on his home office desk, his keys hitting the desk with a soft click. His phone joined it before he frowned and pulled up his messages. One message stopped his movement and he nodded. This was the link after all, the link between the towns. *Emma, you are good. I need to talk to you, but it will have to be tomorrow.* Tonight, he just needed to drop everything and just spend time with his Lord, seeking for peace and answers and rest. His friends were walking the narrowest, most dangerous part of their path, and he knew Brownie wanted to prevent that but just couldn't.

Chapter 40

Two days later, Keegan wandered the downtown area of her new hometown. Brownie's hand held hers tight. He had been seen by the surgeon and given permission to ditch the sling as he called it. He had grinned at her frown.

"Brownie? Someone is following us?" Keegan looked around.

"There is. I've seen Walker and some of the men that I was forced to work with. Obviously some of them were guards and not just lumberjacks." He tugged her with him into a diner. "I need to take you out for lunch."

"You do?" Keegan sighed as she slid into a booth and Brownie slid in beside her. "Now what, Brownie? How do we bring them out into the open?"

"That we will discuss." He looked up with a grin as the waitress greeted him. "Annie, this is my wife, Keegan."

Annie grinned in response.

"Just who you needed, Brownie. Welcome, Keegan." She looked around, her voice dropping. "You need to go see Rogan. He has information for you."

"No need to go and find me, Annie." Rogan grinned from beside her. "I knew that Brownie was heading this way." Rogan, the pastor at a local mission, slid into the booth across from them, nodding as Annie took his usual order. "Brownie, introduce me to your bride."

"Rogan, this is Keegan. Keegan, this is a friend who runs the mission down here. He's Rogan."

"Hi." Keegan glanced through the two men. "You have information, don't you?"

"I do but first we eat and then pray. You're at a crisis right now." His eyes were on Keegan but he saw Brownie nodding.

An hour later, Rogan pointed towards the mission building.

"Let's head inside to my office. I have information locked away that you need."

Keegan spun suddenly, finding herself watched. Walker stood fifteen feet away from her, a smirk on his face. Brownie spun as well, his eyes hardening as Walker tipped an imaginary hat and walked away.

"Brownie? He was that close?" She began to shake in fear.

"He was." Brownie swept her into the building and to Rogan's office. "Rogan, Walker was here. We need to figure out how to get her to safety."

"I don't understand totally what you mean, but here. Let me get you the information and then get you back to your truck."

Aaron turned as the desk sergeant approached him.

"Brownie is here, Aaron. He wants to talk with you."

Aaron moved towards Brownie, who stood near the break room. Keegan stood tight to him, her arms wrapped around herself, definitely feeling out of place. She had not been there before.

"Brownie? What is going on?" Aaron pointed towards a small board room, closing the door to it after then entered.

"Rogan gave me some information that I need to give to you." Brownie bit at his bottom lip. "Walker was around. If Keegan hadn't been close to myself or Rogan, he would have taken her. He was like 15 feet from her."

Aaron's movements stilled as his eyes found Keegan, finding hers shuttered but he could see the agitation and fear in her face.

"What information did he give you?" Aaron's hand was out for the paperwork. He glanced through it, looked around for a chair to pull out, and then grabbed a pen. He read through it numerous times, his pen marking certain points. He sat back at last, his eyes troubled, before he sighed. "Did you read through this, Brownie?"

Brownie nodded, as he watched Keegan closely.

"We did. I don't like what they found. Is that person from town really involved?" Brownie was disturbed about the name.

Keegan stared around before she spoke.

"The man from my town? He's a cousin of that man. That's your connection. And I think Kat had determined that he was related to Walker."

"Is that correct?" Aaron sat back, a finger tapping at the paperwork. He pulled the papers towards him, searching through it. "I don't see that in here."

"No, we have it at home. Kat was specific with what she said. She didn't send it in an email. Instead, she couriered it to me." Keegan's head went down on the arms that she had folded on the table. Her shoulders shook with the tears she was trying hard to suppress.

Brownie's arms were around her as he prayed for his bride. Then he glared at Aaron, finding his glance somewhat amused as he returned Brownie's look.

"I'll come with you to get it. Where's your truck?"

"Right outside. Aaron, this is enough. I want this over now. How close are you to arresting them?"

"A day or so. We're working on the search and arrest warrants right now. So are the detectives in Keegan's hometown. Her parents are still tucked away and providing information." Aaron's smile grew sad. "I'm sorry, Keegan, that you had to go through all this. Your parents are wanting to meet with you but they are not sure what kind of reception to expect."

"Yeah, well, there's that too. I don't know what to expect either." Keegan was on her feet, heading for the door, not aware of what would await them before they reached the home that they shared.

———

Chapter 41

Keegan stared around the town as Brownie drove towards home, Aaron following him. She didn't feel safe. Something was about to happen and she was suddenly afraid. Brownie was attentive, his eyes flickering between the road ahead and around him.

"Brownie? Where is he? He's here somewhere, isn't he?" Keegan's voice was fear filled.

"I know he is. I just can't see him." He looked behind, not seeing Aaron's car. "Where did Aaron go? He was just there." He spun his wheel and headed back that way, still not seeing Aaron's car. He tossed his phone to Keegan. "Call him. I'm heading back to the department."

Slamming on the brakes, Brownie stared at Aaron's car. It sat against the curb, the front doors open. Aaron was missing. He sat for a moment, then reached for the door lock, locking all the doors.

"Brownie? Where's Aaron?" Keegan twisted and turned, trying to find him.

"I don't know. Someone's got to him." Brownie hit the accelerator, taking off before Keegan could say anything more. Only, he didn't make it far before vehicles surrounded him and tried to stop him.

"Brownie!" Keegan's scream of fear echoed in the cab of the truck.

"Hang on!" Brownie spun the wheel, mounted the curb and took off into a parking lot, driving through and out the other entrance and then speeding for the department. He punched in his code at the gate and then drove to park at the back of the lot. Throwing open his door, he ran around and yanked Keegan from the truck, heading for the back door on the run.

Justin looked up startled as Brownie appeared at his door, out of breath. He glanced at Keegan and drew in a breath at the utter terror on her face.

"Brownie? What is going on?" Justin was on his feet, his hands planted on his desk.

"Aaron's disappeared. We were heading to our place with him behind us. His car is sitting at the side of the road but he's gone." Brownie spun in a circle before he reached for Keegan. "Walker was around. Did he get him?"

Justin walked away after pointing Brownie and Keegan to chairs in his office. He was worried, no scared, he thought. This could go bad so quickly, he thought.

"Send out patrols. Aaron is missing and I think he was taken by the ones after Brownie and Keegan."

Stunned silence met his words and then sudden scrambling sent officers searching. Two officers headed towards Justin's office, sent there with instructions not to leave the couple. Brownie looked up at that and nodded. His prayer rose for the officers searching for Aaron and for Aaron himself.

———

Two days passed. The other investigators were prepared to serve the search and arrest warrants. Only the one in charge was missing. They couldn't find him anywhere in town. Brownie nodded when they told him this, just stating that was what he had expected.

Keegan paced the house, worried beyond what she had ever been about Aaron. Who had him and where was he? She turned as Brownie approached, reaching for him, needing the comfort that he could bring her.

"Where is he, Brownie?" Her voice was muffled against him.

"I don't know, sweetheart. I don't know. I pray that he is still alive."

"How can we find him? Justin won't let us out, not without our escort." Keegan was disgruntled at that.

"I know, but we need to." Brownie began to pace, his phone out to call Evan. "Evan? What are you up to today? Are you working? You're not? What about Shay and Tag? They're not. Oh, I see Dougal is here as well as Storm. What did you do? Call in everyone?"

Evan laughed. "No, they volunteered to help. We heard that Aaron is missing and we're heading out to search. Our ladies are heading your way."

"Okay. We'll see them soon. I just wish I could be out there."

"You can't. Walker is waiting for that. And so is his boss. We know who he is. I have a good idea where he's holed up. Abe said his team was heading that way along with some of our officers."

"Okay. Just keep me in the loop." He pocketed his phone, turning to Keegan. "The guys are heading out looking. Abe's team is as well. The ladies are heading our way." He bit at his lip, a new habit of uncertainty that he had picked up.

"Ladies? Okay, we'll work with them, trying to solve this. I am so afraid, Brownie, afraid that Walker or whoever it is will catch up with us before they're arrested and that they will kill us."

"That we can do. They'll be here shortly. Now, where do we work?" Brownie looked around, not quite sure what he should be doing, feeling lost for a moment.

"The office." She headed for the kitchen, opening the fridge and then the freezer. "We'll need food, Brownie, but we don't have a lot." She was almost in tears, the stress of it all briefly overcoming her.

Brownie swept her into his arms, a prayer raising for them and for the investigators. He turned as he heard a knock at the door, suddenly afraid.

Keegan stared at him and approached the door, looking through the door. She didn't recognize the man standing there and turned to Brownie.

"Brownie, who is this?"

Brownie stared through the window before he reached for the door and opened it.

"This is Doug Foster, a friend and fellow officer. And his wife, Darcy. Hi! What brought you two here?"

Darcy shared a look with Doug and then spoke.

"You two did. I have a profile for you, but I hear that Aaron has gone missing?"

"He has." Brownie looked past them. "And our ladies are here."

"They are?" Doug turned. "You have all five of them."

"We do. The guys are looking for Aaron and whatever else it is that they are up to. And you? What exactly are you planning on doing?"

Doug just grinned, turning to greet the ladies.

Chapter 42

Brownie turned from the ladies as they poured over the material and motioned to Doug, pointing to the kitchen.

"They're so engrossed in what they are working through. Let's get them a meal." Brownie stared into the fridge. "Unfortunately, we don't have a lot of stuff."

Doug shrugged, not concerned at all.

"Darcy bought some stuff. Let me go get it." He was out of the house and back, bags of food on the counter. "She has fresh bread, cold meat, salads, and some goodies from a friend of ours who has an Irish bakery."

"That sounds good." Brownie started his preparation before his hands slowed. A thoughtful look crossed his face. "Doug? Who would you suspect? I know that you had an adventure that almost killed Darcy."

"We did. And it was law enforcement who was the one responsible. I don't get that impression with you two though."

"I don't either. I haven't spoken with her parent yet, but Aaron has and he shared what he could. Not a lot, unfortunately. We still have to meet with them but that won't happen for a bit." He turned

213

as he heard footsteps and Keegan appeared. "Keegan?"

"I know who it is. It's not who we thought. He's not related to us, but he is a bigwig in town." She held out a paper that was shaking violently. "He has a huge mill that produces wood chips. He could very easily mill the valuable trees after hours and no one would ever know."

Brownie reached for the violently shaking paper

"He is?" Brownie looked at the paper before he handed it to Doug. Keegan moved into his arms and hugged him tight.

"I'm scared, Brownie. I am really scared. I can see why he took Dad, to hide his illegal accounts. Does that mean Dad will be charged?"

"No, it won't." Brownie sighed as his phone kept chiming. Keeping an arm around Keegan, he reached for it, read his text and breathed a sigh of relief. "Abe found Aaron and is on his way to the hospital with him."

"Thank God!" Keegan was away, her voice carrying back to the two men.

"He's alive?"

"He is. Abe hasn't said much but I didn't expect him to. Now, we need to solve this, figure out how to trap the man and then go on with our lives. This is really drawing the life from Keegan."

"I can see that." Doug paced for a moment before he returned to help plate the sandwiches and treats and then head for the office. "We need to take a break, ladies, and then do some praying and some planning."

An hour later, an hour filled with teasing and laughter, Keegan reached for hands, joining the group into a circle.

"We need to pray. Aaron is alive but we don't know how badly he has been hurt. And I know we have determined who it is that is involved. But we need to plan." She shot a look at Brownie. "Who do we involve from the force?"

"Justin for one. Grayson for another. And then some of the patrol officers. We'll go on the offensive, starting tomorrow." Brownie looked around. "Doug? You said that you were off tomorrow?"

"I am. And Darcy is available. Your guys are free?"

"They are. They have already said that."

"And Abe will be here with his whole team."

Darcy looked up at that point from her phone.

"Frankie is on his way as is Gideon and Dave." Darcy grinned. "This guy has no idea what he's facing."

"As long as it's all legal and he can be arrested, we're good with that." Brownie looked around. "You two can use the cabin at the back for tonight."

"Thank you. Now, we need to plan. Can we get whoever it is we need from your force?"

Brownie nodded, waving his phone.

———

"Justin and Grayson are on their way. And Aaron is being released. He was roughed up but is otherwise okay." He searched for Keegan, finding her watching him, a relieved look on her face. "Today, we finish our plans. Tomorrow, we set them into motion."

Keegan moved slowly through their home that evening, exhausted beyond anything that she had ever imagined she could be. Brownie? He was hurting, she knew, in many ways. He had finally nodded as she had shaken the pain medication at him and given in to her request that he take some. He was now stretched out in bed, sound asleep, but it was a restless sleep. She watched as he tossed and turned, knowing that somehow he was reliving what they had gone through and worried about what they faced.

Smiling sadly, Keegan moved back towards the kitchen, her bare feet seeming to barely touch the floor. She had enjoyed meeting the ladies and working with them, knowing that the ladies from this area would become good friends. Shared, similar circumstances drew them together in a bond. God had provided her with friends who knew what she was going through.

She stood in the kitchen, staring out of the window, the lights off in the house. She frowned as she saw movement at the back of the yard and nodded, knowing that Walker and hi minions were around, trying to find a way in. Only they wouldn't. A man who Brownie called Joseph had been around that day, tightening up their security system. He had grinned at her, simply stating that it was what he did. Keegan had frowned at him even as Doug had stood beside her, telling her that he was one of Abe's security team and this is what he did.

Sighing, Keegan returned to the bedroom, standing for a moment before she slipped in beside Brownie, finding herself wrapped in his arms. Then she slept, a prayer on her lips and rising from her heart that tomorrow would end it all. Only, she didn't know how it end, whether they would still be living by that time tomorrow. Only God knew the path that they had chosen to walk on the morrow and only His protection would keep them alive.

Chapter 43

Brownie stood in the conference room at the department, his arm around Keegan as he watched the commotion in front of him, organized that it was, but still commotion. Abe Finlay stopped beside him, assessing the young couple, and nodded. They were ready to do this, Abe thought. His mind wandered back to what he and Emma had faced as had all of his team members and many friends. He wished it could be different but he knew only too well that this is what had to happen.

Aaron approached Brownie, not feeling quite himself. He had been forced to the side of the road that day, a gun appearing at his window. His hands raised, he had shoved open his door and then was pulled from his vehicle forcibly and shoved into another one. Aaron frowned. He had not been relieved of his weapon when his hands had been handcuffed behind him. He had been held in a rundown building on the edge of town. He hadn't been mistreated too much, just roughed up a bit but unable to escape until someone had walked in and walked out with him.

Brownie turned as Aaron stopped on the other side of Keegan and nodded at him. Aaron shouldn't be there, he thought, but he would be, just to finish off what he had started with them. He watched as Aaron moved towards the table, reaching for the file folders laying on it, leafing quickly through them as he listened to Justin. *Yes,* he thought, *we're ready to go. Now, let's get this show on the road and catch the people involved.*

Pulling out his phone, Aaron moved away from the room to take a call. He thoughtfully slipped his phone away, a nod coming as he processed the information. The man who was involved from Keegan's town? Rolly Winters? He had been arrested early that morning driving drunk and was being processed with the charges that he faced. And he faced many, not just for what he had done to Brownie and Keegan and to Keegan's parents.

Brownie paused beside him, a questioning look on his face. Keegan was with the ladies for now, meeting for prayer. He knew she was still uncertain as to whether they were making the right choice. She had been vocal with him that morning, not backing down when he tried to reassure her. He grinned to himself at the fierce looks that she kept throwing at him before he simply hugged her. Her personality was starting to emerge once more and he loved her spunkiness. As his parents and sister had told him many times, Keegan was just who Brownie needed and why hadn't he found her before.

"Aaron?" Brownie's voice broke through the silence.

Aaron's head shook for a moment before he turned to Brownie, not quite sure how to read him that morning.

"They've arrested Rolly Winters from Keegan's town. On a drunk driving charge but he won't be out for a while. They're processing all the charges."

"That's a relief." Brownie scrubbed at his face, suddenly fearing for what the day would bring. "We're all set?"

"We are. I wish that there was a better way than to put the two of you out there." Aaron grimaced at his words.

"There isn't. We talked it through, planned it, but God is in control. Before we go out, I just want to say thanks, Aaron, for all that you have done. You've been a great friend and support through all of this."

"Thanks, Brownie. It worries me that you're not back to your full strength."

"I know, but it is what it is." Brownie turned and walked away, looking for Keegan, and then with her hand tight in his, walked from the department and headed on a walking tour of the town, knowing full well that Walker was watching them.

The plan had been that while Walker was tracking Brownie and Keegan, other detectives and officers would move in on his employer and the men and women that he had working for him in that town. Aaron prayed that it would work, watching as Abe's team moved out around Brownie. They were not known in town and would just seem to be tourists.

Keegan was a lot more worried than she showed. Walker was behind them, that she knew, just waiting for an opportunity to approach and take them captive once more. If he did that, she knew that neither of them would live. He had promised that at one point during their captivity. She sighed even as Brownie's hand tightened on hers. Just where it would all lead? She had no idea. Keegan's thoughts were momentarily distracted to her parents. How would they get along now, she wondered? There had been so many years, so many bad feelings on her part for what she had thought was their abandonment. Walker and whoever it was that he worked for had a lot to answer for. She was determined to end it all that day, even if it meant her death.

Brownie's eyes were roving the area around them. He could feel the danger approaching but not just from what direction. And it was more than one direction, he knew. Abe had been upfront with him. His team would be close but not close enough to prevent the confrontation. That had to happen. Brownie had nodded, knowing that Abe was correct. Only he didn't want it to happen. He didn't want his sweetheart hurt and that was a real possibility.

He felt Keegan's steps slowing as they approached the mission before she stopped, tugging him to a stop as well. His eyes dropped to her face, seeing her staring straight ahead of him. His peripheral vision caught sight of some of Abe's team and some of his fellow officers moving into a ring around him. This is it, he thought, and frantically sent up prayers for protection and peace.

Keegan stared at the man in front of her. Walker stood there, unkempt in appearance. The last few days had not gone well for him. He had been ordered by his boss to find the couple and bring them to him. Dead or alive, he didn't care which. Walker had been camped out behind Brownie's home, thinking that he could nab them when they came to the back of the yard. Only they never did that. Now,

he had them almost in his clutches and no-one would
stop him.

Chapter 44

Her hand gripping Brownie's tighter, Keegan stared at the man who had held them captive and had tormented them now for weeks. He didn't look so well dressed and well kept any more, she thought. She felt Brownie moving slightly beside her, his stance widening as he assessed the situation. Keegan had no fear. Not any more. The monster, as she called him, was now in front of her. This was when it would end. Would they both be alive or one or both be dead? *Please, dear Lord, spare my pathfinder, my groom, the love of my life. Don't let him be hurt because of me again.*

Walker sneered and then approached her, a smirk on his face. He stopped just short of her, not lifting his eyes to look around him. He didn't see the security team and the officers moving in to encircle them, ready to arrest him. Aaron stood just behind him, his eyes not leaving the man who he called his nemesis.

"Well, well, well. Look who we have here." Walker spoke at last, a sneer in his voice.

"Walker. I can't say that it's a pleasure." Sarcasm dripped from Keegan's voice even as Brownie frowned. She was up to something and hadn't let him know. "Why?"

"Why what?" Walker was canny, not ready to share why he had done what he had done. That would come, he thought, when he had her away from Brownie and on her own.

"Yeah, why? I know you're working for someone. And those someones are from my town and from here. So, again, why? What was in it for you? Other than money and a sense of owning people that you had no right to do."

"Well, little lady, it's like this." Walker decided that he was going to tell her, not realizing that one of Abe's men had pulled out a video camera and was taping it all. "Your mother? She was supposed to share her inheritance with us and didn't. She owes me and you're the reward."

"Inheritance?" Keegan was genuinely puzzled. "Mom had no inheritance coming to her. At least not that I know of and she or Dad would have told me." Her eyes narrowed. "And just where did you put them all these years? Did it really accomplish anything? Did you get what you wanted? I highly doubt that."

"I did. I kept your parents and you separate. I watched you all grieve. Only you never broke." Walker was puzzled by that, not sure why that had been. "Your father will face many charges of theft and money laundering. He won't see the light of day again. And your mother? Who cares what happens to her?" He flicked a hand in dismissal, not seeing the start that Keegan gave.

"Somehow, I don't think so. Tell me, Walker. What all were you involved in? I would really like to know. Other than theft of valuable lumber."

Brownie watched closely, his heart in his mouth, as he listened to Keegan baiting the man. What was she up to, he thought? Keegan, sweetheart, what is your plan that you didn't let us in on?

Walker paused, his eyes narrowing as he watched her before he glared at both her and Brownie.

"Why would you want to know? It's none of your business."

"Sure it is. So, tell me what all is it?" Keegan refused to back down. "Why me? Why did you take me captive at that time?"

Walker sneered once more.

"The time was right. We were to break you and then hand you over to our employer. Only you escaped." He was puzzled at how they had managed that. Davis had never told him.

"So, what all are you involved in?" Keegan kept her eyes on him, wanting answers but not sure that she would ever receive any.

"Okay, then. You're not going to live to tell anyone." Walker had never raised his eyes from her face. "Human trafficking. Money laundering. Theft of valuable material. Drug running."

"And I would suspect murder, assault, threatening, intimidation. What else?" Keegan saw the camera that she thought it was Micah was holding and breathed a sigh of relief. Good, she thought, we have proof.

Walker sneered and then lunged for her, his hands grasping for her neck. Brownie spun with her in his arms and ran from that area, men and women surrounding them as they were rushed from the area. Slamming to the ground, Walker yelled in rage, scrambling to his feet, intent on finding Keegan and Brownie. His rage was to the point that he didn't even realize that his arms were tight in the grasp of officers and handcuffs were being snapped around his wrists. His rage came out in his voice as he yelled for Keegan to come back. Walker struggled to escape, head butting two of the officers before he was wrangled into a patrol vehicle.

Breathing hard, Aaron stepped back and stared at Walker through the car window. They had him and with Micah's help, a confession of sorts. He nodded at the officer to drive away and he turned, finding Abe and Micah standing beside him.

"Here you go, Aaron. I hope this does help." Micah handed over the SD card.

"I am sure it will. The prosecutors will be glad to have this."

"Brownie and Keegan are safe. We were able to get them away with the help of his fellow officers. They'll be at the department for you." Abe paused, not sure how to continue. "Do you need us for anything more? We can stay."

"We'll need to get statements from you and then I think you'll be able to go. It's been a crazy day and not over yet."

Brownie wrapped Keegan tight in his arms, his head down on hers as he stood in the break room at the department. His breath came in gasps as he struggled to regain it. His eyes were closed as he tried to take in what had just happened.

Keegan struggled to get free, standing back from him, shock on her face.

"What just happened? Did we really do that?"

Brownie gave a quick grin.

"We did. Walker is in custody. That's why we were rushed away." He looked up as Aaron appeared. "Aaron?"

"It's over, Brownie. Keegan. It's all over. We have the head one here. Jerry Walker. A cousin of sorts of Walker. He's high here in the county government. That's how they go away with all that. He's facing numerous charges, including fraud at his workplace. He's a nasty person. I am so thankful that God kept you two safe."

Brownie nodded, knowing that the adrenalin would fade and they would be exhausted.

"I want to take Keegan home."

Aaron nodded, knowing he would have wanted the same.

"Let's get your statements and then you can go."

Chapter 45

Keegan roamed her yard three days later, restless without knowing why. Brownie was inside, she knew, on the phone with Justin, trying to determine when he would be able to return to work. Justin was insistent that he not return for a number of weeks, to let Brownie have time to heal.

She turned as she heard a soft sound, a hand covering her mouth as she stared at the couple standing near her. Keegan blinked and then rubbed at her eyes. It was real, she decided. Her mother and father stood in front of her. She could see Brownie walking towards her, his hand out for hers. Aaron stood behind the couple, a smile on his face.

"Mom? Dad? You're here?" Keegan doubted her eyes.

Randy smiled and nodded.

"We are, Keegan. At long last, we're together." He shared a look with Laura. "We have a lot to catch up on but for now, we're here. And look at you. You have become such a beautiful lady."

Laura's face was covered with her tears. Her hands were up and clenched and unclenched. She wanted so much to hug her daughter but didn't know if it would be welcome.

Brownie watched closely, seeing the love that Keegan's parents were showing but also the fear of being ignored and refused. Keegan looked up at him at that point, a question on her face as she hesitated. He gave a slight nod and felt her relax beside him. Lord, this is hard. Brownie prayed for his sweetheart.

Keegan looked around, her eyes catching Aaron, who nodded as well, a smile on his face.

"Keegan?" Laura's voice held the love she felt for her daughter, as she moved towards her.

"Mom! I missed you!" Keegan just sprang towards her mother, their arms tight around one another, their tears flowing as they sobbed. Randy moved towards them, his arms around his ladies.

Brownie stepped backwards, blinking rapidly, his emotions all over the place. Aaron stood beside him, a hand on his shoulder as he turned his back to the three huddled together. It's over. Brownie thought to himself. *I just pray that I don't lose the love of my life now. We married in such a rush. She says that she loves me and I know that I love her more each day. But what happens now?*

Keegan struggled to escape her parents' arm, fear on her face for a moment, spinning and searching for Brownie. She sprung towards him, to be swept close to him. Her arms tightened around him as she sobbed in relief. He was so afraid that she would make herself sick.

Randy and Laura approached. They knew that Keegan was married and that Brownie was her husband. They had been shocked to hear that. Aaron had tried to prepare them as much as he could but he had not been totally able to prepare them. That was impossible to do.

Brownie looked up, finding Randy and Laura near him. He reached out a hand to shake Randy's, finding instead that Randy and Laura just wrapping their arms around them. Aaron watched and then walked away, standing for a moment to look up.

"You did this, Lord. Thank you. Lead us as we finish up what we need to do." He walked away, knowing that Brownie would call him when he could. He had to finish paperwork and then move on to another case.

Brownie stood late that night, watching Keegan as she sat curled up on the couch. She hadn't retired yet, not wanting to. He simply sat beside her, finding her turning to him.

"You okay?"

Keegan shrugged.

"I'm not sure, love. I am not sure. I never thought I would ever see Mom and Dad again. We have a lot to work through and that will take weeks, if not months. They'll need to find someone to counsel them."

"They will. I am glad that they are alive and back in your life. We'll get there with them." Brownie grew quiet. Words were not necessary between them. They sat, huddled together, their thoughts muddled before Brownie began to pray. The night grew late and morning came, bringing the sunbeams through the open drapes and the sounds of the morning echoing through the air.

Brownie rose, sweeping Keegan into his arms and then tucking her into bed. She sighed softly and then snuggled under the blankets, curling up on her side.

He walked back through the house, feeling as if he was starting off on a new path. He was, he decided. Lord, I have no idea where we're heading, what I will be going. But You do. You have walked that path before.

Eight months later, Brownie opened his front door and toed off his loafers, setting them neatly into the closet. He stretched and then yawned. It had been a long day. He had been back at work for a number of months but he was feeling restless. He didn't want to continue as a patrol officer, but he wasn't sure what he wanted to do. Rogan was trying hard to convince him to join him in the mission, using the counselling degree that he had worked in his spare time to achieve.

Searching the house, Brownie stopped in the kitchen. He could not find Keegan. He didn't think that she was heading anywhere that day, but she might have. He looked in the garage. Her car was there. Therefore, she should be somewhere around.

Keegan stood and watched Brownie as he searched for her. She had heard him enter from where she had been in the laundry room folding towels. She had headed for the bathroom to put them away, not meeting him in the hallway at all.

Brownie spun as he felt eyes on him and then grinned, wrapping arms around his beloved Keegan as she sprang towards him. They stood for a moment before he kissed her thoroughly.

"Have a good day, sweetheart?" Brownie studied her face, seeing the contentment that was there. "I love you so much."

"I love you just as much. And yes, I had a good day. The ladies were around as were our Moms. They're a cray bunch when they get together. How was your day?"

"It was okay. I just don't have the same interest or motivation to do patrol anymore."

"No, you're turning to something else. Will you work with Rogan?" She studied him in turn.

"I'm not sure. It's something that we need to pray over."

"Well, then, I guess this package won't interest you." Keegan grinned as she moved away and then handed him an envelope.

"Keegan? What did you do?" Brownie took the envelope, his eyes on her.

"I didn't do anything. Your mom handed me that and asked that we pray over it. I have no idea what it is. I waited for you to come home." Keegan grew pensive. "I haven't decided on what I want to do yet either."

"No, you haven't." Brownie opened the envelope and pulled out the paperwork. His eyes widened as he saw the name. "The Barnabas Foundation? I wonder."

"The Barnabas Foundation? I've heard of them. What do they want?" Keegan leaned against him as he began to read. "They're offering you a position?"

"They are. I wonder why." Brownie stared at the paperwork and then at Keegan. "You know, this is what we have been praying for. An opportunity to work with people and set them on the right paths for their lives. This would do it." He flipped back through the paperwork, reading it more slowly.

"Do they give us a timeline to let them know?" Keegan was trying to read as well, finally just taking the papers from Brownie and searching through them. "This is odd. They don't give a timeline, just tell us to pray and let them know our decision. That's an odd way to do business."

"It's what I've heard that they do. The board there prays over a new opportunity that they want to develop. Once they've made that decision, then they pray for a couple. It is an unanimous decision that they arrive at. Then they approach the couple or person, offer the position, and tell them to pray it over until they reach a decision and then let them know. If the position is refused, then they pray for someone else. I don't know that they have ever had anyone refuse."

"Then, we'll pray. But I certainly feel this is where we're being led. You're not happy being on patrol anymore. You're afraid at times about reacting wrong." Keegan dropped the paperwork on the table and reached to hug him.

"I am, sweetheart. I am. I worry about you when I'm gone, whether we really did find everyone."

"Aaron called today. They found everyone, so you can let that go. He also said that they all took plea deals, so we don't have to testify. And they are wanted in more than this area."

Brownie nodded as he stood for a moment, studying the lady in front of him. Lord, You have blessed me with a helpmeet, someone I needed but didn't know that I did.

"We'll pray over this, but I agree that this exactly what we wanted. Dad asked me the other day what I really wanted to do. I just shrugged. He called me a pathfinder and told me to find the path I was to walk." Brownie grew silent, content to hold his love.

Dear Readers

Thank you for choosing the story of Brownie and his lady, Keegan. What path are you walking right now? Is it one of your choosing or God's choosing? He is our Pathfinder, the One who goes before us. In these turbulent times, it is so comforting that we never walk alone. Not one step. One of my Mom's life verses was Proverbs 3:6. I miss my Mom so much.

Another story that the just took over and ran with, bringing in characters and plot lines that I didn't imagine. I joke with a fellow writer about this and she always sends me a photo of a Ferris wheel. They also drew in so many beloved characters from past stories. Of course Abe and his wife, Emma, and their security team just had to wander through. A beloved set of characters.

The characters that have walked in. They are from *His Dreamseekers* (Evan, Tag, Shay, and Dougal), Abe's team from *His Guardians* series, Doug and Darcy from *The Heart of a Lion*. The Barnabas Foundation is featured in *The Barnabas Chronicles*.

God bless each one of you.

Ronna